A VILLA IN SICILY:

OLIVE OIL AND MURDER

(A Cats and Dogs Cozy Mystery—Book One)

FIONA GRACE

Fiona Grace

Fiona Grace is author of the LACEY DOYLE COZY MYSTERY series, comprising nine books (and counting); of the TUSCAN VINEYARD COZY MYSTERY series, comprising six books (and counting); of the DUBIOUS WITCH COZY MYSTERY series, comprising three books (and counting); of the BEACHFRONT BAKERY COZY MYSTERY series, comprising six books (and counting); and of the CATS AND DOGS COZY MYSTERY series, comprising six books.

Fiona would love to hear from you, so please visit www.fionagraceauthor.com to receive free ebooks, hear the latest news, and stay in touch.

BOOKS BY FIONA GRACE

LACEY DOYLE COZY MYSTERY
MURDER IN THE MANOR (Book#1)
DEATH AND A DOG (Book #2)
CRIME IN THE CAFE (Book #3)
VEXED ON A VISIT (Book #4)
KILLED WITH A KISS (Book #5)
PERISHED BY A PAINTING (Book #6)
SILENCED BY A SPELL (Book #7)
FRAMED BY A FORGERY (Book #8)
CATASTROPHE IN A CLOISTER (Book #9)

TUSCAN VINEYARD COZY MYSTERY
AGED FOR MURDER (Book #1)
AGED FOR DEATH (Book #2)
AGED FOR MAYHEM (Book #3)
AGED FOR SEDUCTION (Book #4)
AGED FOR VENGEANCE (Book #5)
AGED FOR ACRIMONY (Book #6)

DUBIOUS WITCH COZY MYSTERY
SKEPTIC IN SALEM: AN EPISODE OF MURDER (Book #1)
SKEPTIC IN SALEM: AN EPISODE OF CRIME (Book #2)
SKEPTIC IN SALEM: AN EPISODE OF DEATH (Book #3)

BEACHFRONT BAKERY COZY MYSTERY
BEACHFRONT BAKERY: A KILLER CUPCAKE (Book #1)
BEACHFRONT BAKERY: A MURDEROUS MACARON (Book #2)
BEACHFRONT BAKERY: A PERILOUS CAKE POP (Book #3)
BEACHFRONT BAKERY: A DEADLY DANISH (Book #4)
BEACHFRONT BAKERY: A TREACHEROUS TART (Book #5)
BEACHFRONT BAKERY: A CALAMITOUS COOKIE (Book #6)

CATS AND DOGS COZY MYSTERY
A VILLA IN SICILY: OLIVE OIL AND MURDER (Book #1)
A VILLA IN SICILY: FIGS AND A CADAVER (Book #2)

CHAPTER ONE

Being a vet meant dealing with a lot of strange creatures.

Not the patients.

No, the patients were cute, cuddly, adorable, the reason Audrey Smart had gotten into this career in the first place. Audrey had never met an animal she didn't like.

It was the ones paying the bills, and her salary, she could've done without.

Audrey stared at her latest patient's "mummy." The woman stroked her adorable teacup poodle's lolling head and kissed it with her painted, Botoxed lips. "I don't know what's wrong with Donut. He's never this lethargic!"

Hmmm, I wonder. It wouldn't have anything to do with mummy, would it?

Fighting to keep her eyes level, though they were practically itching in their sockets to roll to the ceiling, Audrey explained, once *again,* "You left wine out during your garden party, Mrs. Marx. You said the dog drank half a glass? That's a lot for a little thing like him."

Audrey didn't want to judge, but sometimes, it was so *easy.*

The woman's over-tweezed eyebrows tented. "Nonsense. Donut has very sophisticated tastes, and I only serve the best."

Pushing her ponytail over her shoulder, Audrey brought the stethoscope over the animal's side, listening to the slow murmur of his heart. Poor thing. She rubbed his tiny little head, right between his ears. "I'm sure you have great taste, but even the *best* is not advisable for a dog, since grapes can be toxic. Wine and dogs? Don't mix."

The woman tapped the heel of her Louboutin impatiently on the waxed floor, a defiant look on her pinched, unnaturally bronze face. "You don't know Donut."

Audrey smiled at the little dog as he gazed up at her gratefully, adoringly. "We should induce vomiting."

Her jaw dropped. "You will do no such thing! Vomiting?"

"Okay, well, he's not in any danger. If you'd rather, we can just let him rest. He should be all right in a couple hours, but we'll keep him here for observation."

1

Instead of agreeing, the woman fisted her hands on her hips. "Where's that kind, handsome veterinarian? With the piercing blue bedroom eyes? I demand to see him."

Audrey sighed. Maybe she'd been a little too brusque. But that always happened. She considered herself the voice of these animals she cared for, their champion. Sometimes she couldn't help being insensitive to their owners. "Dr. Ferris is not here. I'm the veterinarian on staff now."

She gave Audrey a thorough eye-scraping, as if to say, *Says who?* "I demand to see a *real* doctor."

Another sigh. At thirty-two, she shouldn't have had to tote around her veterinary school diploma as an accessory along with her iPhone. Maybe it was just good (or bad) genes that still made her look like she wasn't yet out of college, or that she was a woman, or that most of the pet owners who came to Back Bay Animal Care in downtown Boston were too obsessed with their own selves to be observant of her *Dr. Audrey Smart* nameplate, but seriously. How many times did she have to deal with this?

Three times this *week*, apparently.

Biting her tongue, she grabbed her iPad from the examination table and reached for the door. When she opened it, she motioned to one of the vet techs to see to making Donut comfortable with the other animals in observation. "I'll put a note for Dr. Ferris to take a look when he begins his shift in the morning."

Finally appeased, Mrs. Marx gave her poor, inebriated dog some kisses and said, in baby-talk, "Mummy'll miss you so much!" Then she glared at Audrey as she swept past her, carrying a choking cloud of perfume with her. "See that you do," she said, chin up like some member of British peerage, already sifting through her enormous designer purse for her wallet.

The second Audrey showed the woman out the door, she shed the plastic smile she'd been struggling to keep on her face. She checked the time on the clock above reception. Three minutes until quitting time. *Finally.*

Heading for the break room, she'd already begun to unbutton her white coat when a wall of trouble sprouted up in front of her.

There was nowhere to escape to. If he hadn't already spotted her, she'd have ducked into one of the examination rooms, but as it was, they were alone in the hallway. Dr. Brice Watts was one of those people who carried angst and drama everywhere he went. He was like a

2

tornado, absorbing everything in his path, only to spit it out, a shadow of what it once was.

"Listen, *Aud,* girl," he said, strolling down the hall toward her, winking in the general direction of the reception desk, probably at one of the few vet techs he hadn't already added to his list of conquests. "Can you cover for me tonight? I got a *thing.*"

He added air quotes, after the fact. The guy was forever air-quoting everything, whether it needed it not.

"A thing?" Audrey repeated, using her own air quotes for, "Like a *plantar wart?*"

He laughed at her like she was a mildly amusing child who'd overstayed her welcome with the adults. Mid-forties, spare-tired, and balding, yet he played the *I'm better than you* act so well that a lot of people, surprisingly, bought in. "Tickets to a performance at Boston Symphony Hall. Mahler."

"Sorry, *Bri,* boy," she said with a shrug, deriving a little too much pleasure from the nickname. "But I've got a *thing,* too."

His face fell. She'd clearly surprised him, considering of all the doctors on staff, she was the one who was almost always, reliably, free. "Need I remind you, you're the low man on the totem pole here?"

She stared at him. It wasn't the first time he'd dropped some last-minute bombshell on her toes, forcing her to completely upend her important Netflix-watching schedule.

"I understand. But I also know that I've had this engagement planned for months, and I can't break it last minute. I'm sorry. Besides, I took your emergency call shift last week, for your other *thing.* Remember?"

From the look on his face, he didn't.

"Remember? That gala at the Boston Ballet you *had* to go to?"

"Ah, *that.* Yes, but—"

Audrey made like she was checking her watch, even though she wasn't wearing one. "Like I said, I've got to be somewhere."

She squeezed past him in the hall, leaving him grumbling behind her. At her locker, she grabbed her things, hoping she could escape to the T without other fires popping up.

It wasn't like she'd made it up. She really *did* have somewhere to be. But she had a feeling that with her luck, it'd be even more painful than marinating in Mrs. Marx's noxious company for a fifteen-minute appointment.

*

3

Growing up, Audrey had dreamed about coming home to a welcome committee. She'd open the door and a half-dozen of her favorite beings on earth would be there, tails wagging excitedly, waiting for their cuddles. She'd wanted a dog or two, a cat definitely, maybe a rabbit and a hamster. Even a turtle, just to round things out.

That idea went down the toilet when she graduated from veterinary school nearly two hundred thousand dollars in debt, got a job, and tried to enter the *real world,* four years ago.

The only place she could afford in the city was a little walk-up closet in Southie, the insides of which had probably seen yellow crime scene tape more than once. She'd been happy, though, excited at the prospect of starting this chapter of her life as a career woman.

It was only after she moved in that she noticed the part of the lease that said *No pets.*

Not that it would've been fair to her brood, if they existed. She worked way too many hours nowadays, anyway, chipping away at her student loans.

Sighing, she stepped into the crypt-quiet apartment and looked around at the dreary gray walls. She'd fixed the place up as best she could, giving it homey touches, trying to make it hers, but it still screamed *temporary.*

Her eyes fell upon a white envelope on the floor. Someone must've shoved it under the door.

As she reached for it, her first thought was, *Secret admirer?*

Then she laughed at her stupidity. She didn't just *look* twenty. Some of her thoughts, she realized, were equally as naïve. Especially the ones regarding men. There was a guy on the fourth floor, below her, who was kind of cute, but even at thirty-two, Audrey couldn't do more than blush like a schoolgirl whenever they ran into each other on the stairs. One time, he asked her if she knew of any good Thai places nearby, and she'd just giggled maniacally. He must've thought she was a moron.

Lifting up the flap of the envelope, she groaned when she saw the logo for her landlord's holding company. "What do they want? I'm not underwater on my rent," she muttered, unfolding the letter.

She only scanned it at first. Then she read the whole thing. Twice. Then, stomping into the kitchen, she threw it down on the table and desperately wished for something furry to pet.

The nerve of those people, selling the building on her, without notice! Not only that, the new owners, *doubling* the rent! Wasn't there some kind of law against that?

She grabbed her phone, breathing hard, trying to think of someone to call, but then she noticed the time.

In an hour, she'd be expected at the Copley Square Hotel for her high school reunion.

Her past experience with high school reunions hadn't been stellar. Her five-year had been a big bust. She'd gotten all dolled up, excited to tell people that she'd graduated *magna cum laude* from BC and was on her way to veterinary school, and then ... nothing.

No one even noticed her. She'd spent the entire time at her table, alone. Someone had mistaken her for a waitress and ordered a whiskey sour from her.

It had been so bad, she'd said a big *hell no* to her tenth. And she'd been firmly in favor of shunning the fifteenth, twentieth, twenty-fifth ... every last one of them.

That is, *until* ...

She opened her phone to the last message Michael Breckenridge had sent her on Facebook a couple days ago. *Can't wait to see you, cutie.*

A frisson of pure teenage excitement traveled down her neck. Michael had been her biggest crush, all through high school, the guy she could barely look *near* without sending her heart racing and her cheeks flushing. A year older, he'd been part of the thespians. His performance of Willy Loman in *Death of a Salesman* had brought down the house at Westwood High.

He'd connected with her, completely out of the blue, a few weeks ago, when she'd joined a Facebook group to keep abreast of the reunion plans. Amazingly, he'd remembered her, even though all Audrey had ever done was scenery.

Cutie.

She shivered as she ran for the shower, trying to remember the last time she'd been complimented like that. Really, never. Unfortunately, her fifth-year reunion was a perfect reflection of her dating life as a whole.

Completely uneventful. Nonexistent. A total dud.

This time, things would be not only different, but *magical*.

Audrey, be proud. It's been fifteen years. You're a doctor of veterinary medicine.

Forty-five minutes later, she finished applying her fake eyelashes and stood back, smoothing out her body-hugging, ruby red dress. The clerk at Nordstrom had said it was killer, and it'd drawn a small crowd of admirers, complimenting her slim figure and flawless skin. So what if they were all over eighty? Audrey peered in the mirror at herself and pushed back her shoulders. It was so bare, so *sexy,* hardly more than a slip. She'd never worn anything like this in public before.

You look stunning, she told herself, echoing the ladies in the dressing room as she pulled a few dark tendrils from her updo.

She applied bombshell-red lipstick, the finishing touch, smacking her lips together and blowing a kiss to the mirror.

"Michael's not going to be able to take his eyes off you," she whispered to her reflection, *really* wishing she had something furry to pet.

At least, I hope.

Taking a deep breath, she grabbed her purse and headed for the door. As she did, her phone buzzed.

She nearly lost her balance in her four-inch heels as Michael's name appeared on the screen.

CHAPTER TWO

Audrey opened Facebook Messenger and read the message for the tenth time. *Save a seat for me, cutie.*

She threw the fabric of her dress over her knee and remembered exactly why she didn't wear evening gowns with thigh-high slits on public transportation.

A man with a lack of teeth and an abundance of hair—literally, hair *everywhere*—leered at her from across the aisle, making lewd gestures. Was there a full moon out?

Not that she could narrow her weirdo interactions to once a month. They seemed to happen more and more often these days. Last week, a guy with an MIT sweatshirt had leaned over and asked if he could sniff her hair.

Sometimes, she really hated the T. But in addition to almost not having an apartment, another thing she didn't have? Her own mode of transportation. Not even a bicycle.

She buried her nose in her phone, trying to control her rapidly thumping heartbeat.

Save a seat for me, cutie.

Hormonal teenage tingles erupted all over her body as she tried to concentrate on the day's news. But it was all depressing stuff—politics, crime, natural disasters. Nothing even remotely cheery at all. Why did the news always have to be bad?

The worst news of the day: *No apartment.* Seriously, she was already pushing it, trying to pay off her student loans in her little hovel. How was she supposed to pay that kind of rent? This was bad. Bottom-of-a-chasm-bad.

As she swiped with her thumb, she nearly scrolled right past a sun-soaked, stucco villa on a scenic hillside, above a deep blue sea.

She let out an audible sigh, almost feeling the warm Mediterranean heat on her cheeks, cool sea breezes in her hair. Summer in downtown Boston was sweaty, noisy, and gross. She paused and scrolled back to the photograph, smiling wistfully.

A place like that was probably free of all the ills of the world. Politics? What's that? Crime? Not on your life! Natural disasters? Never heard of them! And creepy, leering men probably didn't dwell there, either. It existed away from all of that, in its own little bubble of perfection.

She had to read the headline three times before it finally cracked her cerebrum.

Own a villa in beautiful Sambuca, Sicily for only $1!

Right. There had to be some catch. Something the advertisers weren't saying. *All it will cost you is $1 ... and your living soul!*

Somehow, that ridiculous headline managed to taint paradise ever so slightly.

Nevertheless, it'd done its job. She was intrigued. She clicked on the ad.

It brought up the same photograph of a lovely Italian villa, along with the words, *Have you ever wanted to live in Italy? Now is your chance, at a very affordable price. Today, you can own a piece of beautiful Sambuca, Sicily, for less money than a cup of coffee! Plant your dreams now! See you on this side of your own private Eden!*

Audrey brought the photograph so close to her face, she nearly bumped the screen of her phone with her nose. She kind of did want to dive right into those blue Mediterranean waters. Charter a yacht. Go sailing with a tall, dark Italian named Antonio or Rinaldo. Something ending in an "o."

She sighed again, imagining a walk down a cobbled street to her beautiful Italian villa. It all seemed so quaint, so simple, so ... European.

She almost missed her stop at Copley. But when the doors to the T opened, she looked around her bleak surroundings and a bit of sense leaked back into her head. *There's a reason those homes are only a dollar, Audrey. If something looks too good to be true, it usually is.* Her sensible mom's voice filled her head, the same woman who'd never let Audrey stand at the bus stop without an umbrella if it even smelled like drizzle.

She stood up, arranging her slit modestly and, ignoring the hairy man's catcalls, exited the car. It wouldn't have been too hard to make it to Copley Square Hotel had she not been wearing lethal heels. *People actually walk in these?* she wondered as she got one stuck for the thousandth time. Sewer grate, crack in the sidewalk, uneven curb ... as an old city, Boston had plenty of those. Her mom would've insisted she wear flats, but Easy Spirits would've totally dulled the effect she was hoping to have on Michael. Somehow, she made it to the hotel with all her limbs intact.

Inside, she tottered a bit to the registration table at the front of the ballroom.

She hadn't seen them in ten years, so it took her a minute to recognize them. Mitzy Silverman, Westwood High's *Most Likely to Earn a Lexus with her MLM Scheme,* with a fruity drink at one elbow and an already-drunk Dobie Something, class quarterback, staring down the front of her dress, at the other.

She giggled at something Dobie said and then scraped her eyes over Audrey. Her smile faded. "This is the Westwood High reunion, dear. Are you sure you're in the right place?"

"I know. Audrey Smart?"

She rolled her eyes. "There is no ..." She stopped when Audrey leaned down and grabbed the name tag, holding it up triumphantly.

"Thanks for all your help!" she called, ripping off the backing and adhering it to her boob.

Heaving a sigh, she wondered if it wasn't too late to make a break for the door. *The Invisible Girl. That's me.*

It made sense that few people recognized her. They'd had over a thousand people in her class, and she'd been a complete wallflower, spending most of her time volunteering at the pet clinic instead of going to school functions.

Then she thought of Michael. *Cutie.*

At first, it might as well have been a room of strangers in ball gowns and budding wrinkles. Then she gradually began to recognize some of them. A mousy girl who used to share her flute stand in band had totally become a knockout. The class burn-out, who'd checked out freshman year, had turned in his flannel for a three-piece suit. Around the room, people chatted about their lives, and Audrey picked up snippets of conversation here and there.

But no one came running to her, arms out, excited to give her a hug, as appeared to be happening all over the room, little volcanoes of *Oh my god!* erupting all around. Her former classmates swerved around her, like she had the word *Plague* stamped on her forehead.

That was all right. She wasn't there for them. Her best friend was her sister, after all, and that was all she needed. At the tables, people she sort-of-maybe-not-quite recognized proudly traded photographs of their children and suburban McMansions and exotic vacations and swapped stories of their exciting lives. Audrey fidgeted, fighting the urge to bolt.

She scanned the room for that signature thick, wayward blond mop of his, that million-dollar Ode to Orthodontia smile. His Facebook photo had been that of Snoopy, so it wasn't much help, but she imagined a more filled-out, sexier version of the old Michael. Men always seemed to age better. Hello, Sean Connery? Really, how much could he have changed in fifteen years? She hadn't changed *nearly* enough, she realized, as her knees actually knocked together. Thank goodness for long dresses.

Taking a deep, cleansing breath, she crossed the ballroom, hearing bits of conversation here and there—a "Just got promoted to CFO!" here, a "Tuscany was enchanting, but I prefer Milan" there.

On the way, Audrey passed by a guy that she almost recognized and did a double-take. He did the same. She stopped. The last time she'd seen him, he'd been doubled over a trash can, too scared to give his valedictorian speech. Back then, he'd had bad acne, an unfortunate crew cut, and a bit of a weight problem. "Kevin?"

"Audrey?" He came up to her and gave her a kiss, then stood back to look at her. She did the same, gaping. The baby fat was gone, his skin flawless, his dark hair tumbling in a rakish way.

"Y-you look great!" she stammered, hardly able to believe it. He'd been her lab partner during her junior and senior years, and the reason she didn't go insane. He'd also been a bit of a nerd—okay, a lot of a nerd—so much so that she'd barely even looked at him. He'd almost asked her out, in a roundabout way, but Audrey had always scurried away whenever he got that amorous look in his eye.

Now, he was gorgeous. Flat-out, Grade A eye candy. She grabbed his arm. "Oh, god, it's so great to see—"

"And this is my wife," he said. "Mimi."

Audrey found herself gaping at the exotically beautiful Asian woman. She was sure she'd seen her on a magazine cover somewhere. "Oh. Um, hi. You look familiar."

Mimi only giggled.

"Could be. She's a former fitness model. But more recently, she's been a physicist who worked on my team. That's how we met." He beamed at her, took her hand, and squeezed.

"Your team?" she asked.

"Oh, yes, my company works with the government, pioneering new technologies which will create clean energies to make a better future for the world," he said, sounding much like a commercial announcer.

"Wow ... so you're literally ... saving the world?"

He nodded. "That's right. What about you?"

Audrey hesitated. Next to that, doctor of veterinary medicine didn't seem all that grand. But what the heck. To some people, their pets *were* their world. She raised her chin with pride. "Well, I'm a—"

Just then, the DJ started playing "Oh What a Night," and his wife pulled on his tuxedo. "Come on, Kevvy. Let's go dance!"

Audrey waved at him as he was dragged away.

Finally, she made it to the bar. The bartender ignored her for the first five minutes, and then finally looked up at her. "Rum and Coke?" she asked. She didn't normally drink, but she desperately needed to take the edge off.

"ID, please?"

She rolled her eyes to the ceiling and pointed to her name tag. When that didn't work, she unzipped her purse and pulled out the ID. "I'm thirty-two," she said to him, wondering when she would start to feel flattered about being mistaken for being under the age of twenty-one.

With her drink in hand, she'd just begun to take a sip through the stirrer straw when someone said, "Ashley?"

At first, she didn't turn around, but when someone said it again, adding her last name, she looked up.

"Audrey, actually," she said to the woman with the short dark pixie cut who smiled at her. She had a flowy scarf around her neck and had the smart, no-nonsense look of a psychoanalyst, but Audrey remembered her. "Kristin?"

She nodded, and Audrey smiled, happy to find another person to talk to so she wouldn't be helplessly alone.

"Yes!" Kristin said. "Wow, you look great. You haven't even changed!"

"Thanks, so do you." It was all coming back now. They'd worked on scenery together, especially for *Death of a Salesman*. They'd both painted the living room fireplace while drooling over Michael as he rehearsed his lines on stage. Part friends, part rivals over Michael's attention, they'd become close only because neither of them had much success in catching the actor's eye. "You still live in the area?"

"No. Moved to New York. We're up here for the weekend, Rob and I. My husband. I met him at NYU. He's a physician in Brooklyn. I run my own non-profit, helping to put an end to human trafficking."

Wow. Yet another person saving the world. It seems my high school class bred them like rabbits. "That's amazing."

"God, it's great to be back, and to see you!" she said, rubbing Audrey's bare arm. "What about you? Are you married?"

"No! But I actually still live in the city. For now, at least. I'm a—"

"Oh my god."

Kristin's eyes had drifted somewhere behind Audrey, and were now bulging.

When she spun around to follow her line of view, sure that a waiter was on fire or zombies were invading or something, she saw him.

He stood in the doorway, at the top of the stairs, pausing there like royalty waiting to be announced. People stopped talking. In her head, the DJ's Backstreet Boys' track screeched to an ear-splitting stop. A small earthquake rippled under her feet, which would've sent her stumbling if she didn't have the bar against her back.

Because there he was …

The Michael Breckenridge.

He scanned the place, eyes falling on Audrey, zeroing in. Target acquired.

And then he started heading right for her.

CHAPTER THREE

"There he *is*," Kristin breathed. "Do you remember how amazing he was as ... what was his name? Willy Lohan?"

"Um ... Loman," Audrey murmured, taking him in. Taking *all* of him in, including the extra hundred and sixty pounds he had with him.

No, Michael Breckenridge hadn't ballooned quite *that* much. Oh, he definitely had the spare tire, a burgeoning extra chin ... but most of the added weight belonged to the tall, Barbie-esque bleached blonde on his arm, drowning in sequins, like she was about to give away a sedan on *The Price Is Right*.

Audrey nearly spit her mouthful of rum and Coke out as he jog-strutted down the stairs, a sassy little swing in his step, like a cross between John Travolta and a motivational speaker. As he did, he snapped his fingers and pointed at different people in his adoring crowd. Caught a few kisses from the girls.

This was clearly a guy who *lived* for his high school reunions.

She squinted, wondering if it was just poor lighting, but were those long, luscious blond locks now the victim of ... gasp! ... a receding hairline?

Before she could make the determination, he deposited the blonde at a table like a Hefty bag on the curb and bee-lined it toward Audrey.

Or ... not toward her. More like, toward the bar.

Unfortunately, as he got closer ... this walking nightmare?

Only got worse.

He was tan, unnaturally so, but the tan didn't hide the massive undereye bags and his Rudolph-red, runny nose. Or the freckles in his complexion and the general droopiness of his jowls. Added to the receding hairline, he looked about, oh ... sixty. He was wearing a rumpled tux, but there was some foreign, greenish substance on his lapel. It could've been guac, snot, or vomit. None of those things seemed particularly appealing to Audrey at the moment.

And yep, definitely a receding hairline. Considering he'd grown his blond locks so long they touched his shoulders, he now looked a little like a swaggering Benjamin Franklin.

"Hey, girls," he said, pointing at them as he sidled up to the bar. Appropriately, the bartender didn't card *him* as he asked, "Open bar?"

When the bartender nodded, he said, "Fantastic," and gave an itemized list, counting off on his fingers.

As the bartender lined them up, he grabbed the first one, a Stella, and chugged it.

Wiping his mouth with the back of his hand, he turned to them, elbow on the bar, and grinned. "Hey … I know you two."

Sure. The two of them had been like peanut butter and jelly during their after-school rehearsals. One was rarely seen without the other. Audrey looked at Kristin, who seemed to have fluttered off onto some cloud, she was so starstruck. It was true, they'd spent hours inhaling paint fumes and fantasizing about the day when Michael Breckenridge would notice them. Despite the fact that their crush now looked like a Founding Father, for Kristin, it looked like that dream was finally coming true. She chirped, sounding no older than seventeen, "Yes, I'm Kristin? From scenery?"

He nodded. "Yeah. Thought so." Then his eyes swung to Audrey. More specifically, Audrey's boobs. "Audrey Smart."

She nodded. At least *he* had the name right.

He leaned into her, his breath reeking of alcohol. His hand snaked around her back, landing on her backside. "Wow, aren't you a little slice of pie."

She winced and looked over at Kristin, hoping to be saved, but Kristin's eyes filled with desperation. "Michael, we were just talking about your legendary performance in *Death of a Salesperson,*" she gushed, wrapping her arm around his elbow. "You really brought down that house."

He'd been leering at Audrey, so uncomfortably close she could count the pores on his ruddy nose, but when Kristin touched him, he looked down at her hand and then at her face, disinterested. "Hey. Rachel Maddow. Scram."

Wounded, Kristin took a sip of her wine and scurried off, thereby driving the final nail into the coffin that was Audrey's pseudo-friendship with her.

He leaned forward, eating up whatever was left of her personal space. "So … *cutie.*"

Before, when written in a Facebook bubble, she'd relished it. Now that he'd said it, nearly spitting it in her ear, it sounded almost … *dirty.*

She managed to skirt away a bit, but came in contact with a wall at the side of the bar, where she could move no farther. He filled the gap, his hot, noxious breath assaulting her skin. She glanced at the table, where his female companion was chatting with the girls around her table, oblivious to Michael's shenanigans. "You came with a date?"

"A date?" He glanced in her general direction. "No. That's just my wife."

Just my wife.

He started to play with the spaghetti strap of Audrey's dress, lifting it playfully and delving his fingers underneath as his eyes roved over her bare skin. She'd read it in romance novels before, but until then, she'd never quite known what "undressing her with his eyes" meant. "We have a, you know ..." He leaned in closer, his lips brushing against her ear, nose burying itself in her hair. "... *open* relationship."

Audrey's jaw dropped. He couldn't be ... he wasn't ...

"And I saw a pretty nice coat closet on the way in. So, baby ...I'm game if you are." He waggled his eyebrows suggestively.

Oh, no. He *was*.

With that realization sending shivers—not the good kind— down her spine, the drink slipped from Audrey's hands, landing on her toes before splattering everywhere.

Michael was too busy staring down the front of her dress to notice.

She really needed a drink right about then, to clear the gag that lodged itself in her throat. Instead, she started to cough, doubling over. Hacking like a lung cancer patient.

Thank goodness, Michael backed away, patting her back a little half-heartedly as Audrey's choking began to attract a small audience, the first one Michael wasn't happy to have. "Something go down the wrong pipe?"

She cleared her throat. "I'm fine. But you're not," she told him. "What happened to you?"

He reached for his drink. "Relax, cutie. Tonight's about fun."

She stared at him.

"And if you aren't game," he continued with a smirk, "I guarantee there are about a hundred other girls in here who would be. So if you're not into this, don't waste my time, all right, babe?"

She mulled the words over, their taste sour on her tongue. "Waste your time?"

He chuckled and winked at a waitress. "Yeah. You heard me."

Before she could even think about whether it was the right thing to do, her heart took over. She grabbed the drink from his hand and tossed it in his face, eliciting a small gasp from a few people around them. "I wouldn't visit the coat closet with you if I were your freaking ski jacket!" she shouted.

And in the next fraction of a second, her reputation as the Invisible Girl was shattered.

Because that's all it took for every eye in the place to suddenly land smack dab on her.

CHAPTER FOUR

Audrey marched right over to the blonde who was "just" Michael's wife and stood in front of her, chest heaving.

"I didn't know your husband was an interior designer," she said.

The woman cast a judgmental eye over her and snapped, "What?"

"He invited me to check out the coat closet with him."

That got the appropriate reaction. The woman's face twisted, and her eyes shifted toward the bar. Clearly, if there *was* an open relationship, "just the wife" didn't know about it. She pushed up from her chair and marched in his direction.

Sense only began to leak back into Audrey's head when she turned and realized that everyone in the place was holding their breath, watching and waiting for World War Three to erupt. Not wanting to witness the casualties, she skittered up the stairs with her head down, still feeling the weight of her entire graduating class's eyes on her back.

It was only when she escaped out to the lobby, behind a potted plant, that she finally took a deep breath. Exhaling, she stared up at the ornate chandelier and let out a little groan. She replayed the last few moments over in her head, cringing mightily as she banged the back of her head gently, rhythmically on the wall.

Michael, who had forever been the stuff of her every dream, her every torrid fantasy ... was a complete and utter piece of crap.

As was most of her life.

This was not how things were supposed to turn out. In high school, she'd accepted her role as the invisible wallflower because she knew that if she kept her head down and studied and made something of herself, eventually, she'd be a success, like Kevin. Wasn't that the formula? Work hard in school so you could impress everyone later. She'd followed it to a T, hoping that by now she would have the husband who adored her, beautiful kids, the enviable career and home. She'd have dozens of stories to tell people about the wonderful life she'd made for herself.

But what did she have now?

Not even one of those things.

At that second, she felt it sliding over her body like a suffocating blanket. The self-pity. Her face contorted into ugly-cry mode. A sob

17

caught itself in her throat, but before she could let it out, she realized that Mitzy was leaning over so she could peer at her from behind the reception table, part disgusted, part amused.

"Are you okay, dear?"

Audrey batted aside the palm fronds that were doing a terrible job of concealing her despair, plastered a smile on her face, and waved. "Just fine, thanks."

"You're not leaving so soon?"

"Oh, yes I am," Audrey muttered, heading for the door and pulling out her phone, wondering if anything in this world could make her feel better.

Thankfully, she knew just who to call.

*

Sabrina was waiting at the door when Audrey limped down the street, her feet two giant blisters. The second Audrey reached the top step, Sabrina deposited a glass of red wine into Audrey's hand. "Bad?"

"Worse," Audrey said with a grateful smile, kicking off her shoes in the foyer and taking a gulp, letting it slip down her throat.

Audrey's older sister had The Life. The Life most people, including Audrey, only dreamed of.

Sabrina was wearing yoga capris, matching sports bra, and a hooded sleeveless jacket. Her white-blonde hair, no roots, was piled in a so-called "messy" bun that looked like it'd taken effort to achieve. Her "relaxation wear" still managed to look more put together than most of Audrey's ensembles. And even though she'd just popped Byron out six months ago, she had nary a stomach pooch to speak of.

Many siblings might have been jealous. Sabrina was the popular one in school, the girl with all the friends, the person to whom good things came easy. Now, she had a brilliant husband, a an IP lawyer whose clients included some of the biggest firms in Boston, the gorgeous brownstone on the swankiest street in the city, and three adorable rug-rats … and yet she still managed to look like one of the Real Housewives of Beacon Hill.

Right now, at her lowest of lows, Audrey should've probably wanted to wring her sister's neck for getting all those things she always wanted but never could attain. But she simply couldn't. Brina was number one on her friends list. The person she'd call if she needed to hide a body. Automatic Maid of Honor, no need to ask the question, if she ever had the fortune of walking down the aisle.

Audrey followed her into her showroom-perfect living room and collapsed on the sectional next to her. For someone with kids, who had absolutely no idea company was coming, she'd kept the place remarkably clean.

But that was Sabrina. All-around perfect, all the time.

Brina pulled her knees under her body and took a sip from her wine glass. "Michael?"

Audrey set her glass of wine on the coffee table, grabbed a brocade pillow, and clamped it over her head.

"I told you."

She had, yes. Wise Sabrina, the Seer of All Things Male.

Unfortunately, Audrey hadn't listened.

Brina knew all about the Michael Breckenridge thing. She'd seen the way Audrey drooled over him when they were in high school. The second Audrey got the text from him, she'd been all in Brina's face, asking what it possibly could mean. In addition to her many talents, Brina could probably have had her own television talk show, *The Man Whisperer*, imparting her sage advice to the clue-challenged Audreys of the world. Brina had explained, in detail, that she should be careful, that it was only a text, that no, this didn't mean that they were destined for one another.

Audrey had listened politely, as she always did whenever her sister talked, and then … completely disregarded everything she said.

As usual.

She'd allowed her thoughts to spiral out, elevating that text to the importance of the Magna Carta. She'd obsessed. She'd planned. She'd actually been planning a destination wedding in some Caribbean paradise.

"One of these days, I need to listen to you," she said, voice muffled by the pillow.

"Duh." Brina reached over and snatched the pillow away from her head. "Come on, tell me. It can't be that bad."

Hair crackling with static, Audrey tried to burrow between the cushions. "Oh, it can be! It's worse. So much worse, Bri. First of all, he was married. Second of all, he only wanted me for a tumble among the coats."

Brina winced. "Seriously?"

"Not to mention that these past fifteen years have been really cruel to him. He'd morphed into Ben Franklin on a bad hair day."

"Really? Wow."

"Also, he's a lush." She grabbed her wine and drained the glass in one swig. "More, please."

Brina complied, pouring her a glass of what was probably the expensive stuff, since that was all they really had around there. She and her husband, Max, were into the "finer things" like that. Not that Audrey knew the difference. She gulped like she was at a keg party.

"Well, at least now you know. You can move on," Brina offered brightly.

Audrey slumped into the sofa, pulling a blanket over her evening gown. This didn't make her feel better. Brina had forever had a long line of suitors to go through, like tissues. For Audrey, there was no one, *nowhere* to move on to. "And I'm going to lose my apartment," she moaned.

"You're what?"

Audrey stuck her lower lip out. "New owners. They're nearly doubling my rent. And I can't afford that and my student loans."

"Oh." Brina patted her heart. "Well, you know you can move in here."

Audrey looked around. "And sleep where? On this sofa? You don't have the room."

"Nonsense. Plenty of room. I'll put the girls together. They'll love to bunk up."

Audrey shook her head. "I'm sure Max would love that."

"Don't be silly! He'd be happy to—"

She stopped when Audrey flashed her a doubtful look.

Max was a nice guy, and they got along, but she wasn't exactly sure she could live under the same roof as him. He was a bit OCD and liked perfection, which was why he loved Brina—and why Audrey knew she'd probably drive him to an early grave. The first and last time he'd visited her apartment in Southie, his eyes did an Indy 500 around her cramped living room, silently judging every dust particle. After five minutes, he'd feigned an allergy attack and told Brina he'd wait outside.

Brina sipped her wine. "Fine. But what else are you going to do?"

"Well, up until precisely an hour ago, I was really holding out hope that Michael and I would fall hopelessly in love, and he'd invite me to move in with him, thus beginning the romance of the century," she said, staring miserably into her now-empty glass.

"Aw. Honey," Brina murmured.

Audrey ran her hands through her hair, shaking out the updo. "I know. I'm stupid. I'll never learn."

Brina pushed off her part of the sectional and sat down next to her younger sister, wrapping an arm around her. "You can move out of the city? The rents are cheaper the farther out you go."

"Not being on call. I need to be close enough to get to the center right away." Audrey put her head on her sister's shoulder and recalled her last moments at work, dealing with Mrs. Marx. She cringed. "I hate it, too. I hate my job."

Brina blinked her long eyelashes. "What? Oh, no you don't! You love those animals. You always have. You were born to be a vet."

"You're right. I love the animals. It's the *people* I could do without. I mean, some of them are okay, but I just get frustrated, and ..." She sighed. "Sometimes I wish I could just pack it all in and start over somewhere else."

"Oh, you don't mean that."

Sabrina launched into a long-winded speech about how Boston was the greatest city in the world, and all her friends and family were here, and if she did move away, she'd miss it. Audrey only heard part of it, because at that moment, the ad she'd seen on her phone while riding the T popped into her mind.

The sun-bleached, cobblestone streets.

The bright blue Mediterranean Sea.

The one-dollar price tag.

All of it, far, far away from this horror show that had become her life.

Meanwhile, Brina droned on. She was just getting to the inevitable part about how important it is for one to learn to count one's blessings, when Audrey straightened up like an exclamation point and grabbed her bag. "I know what I could do!"

Yes, Audrey had concocted many hare-brained schemes before that never worked out, her imagined marriage to Michael Breckenridge just one of them. She probably had a wild, *talk me down from the ledge* look in her eyes, because Brina stopped mid-sentence and uttered a cautious, "Don't tell me ..."

She ripped the phone out of her purse and scrolled to find the ad in her feed. Of course, she couldn't find it, now that she wanted it. "It was here ... somewhere ..."

"This isn't another Tinder date, is it? That last one was a serial killer in the making. What was his name, Bruce? He looked straight out of *Silence of the Lambs*."

"No. Of course not." Though part of her had to admit, this probably wasn't much saner.

"What?" Brina leaned forward and peered over her shoulder. "You really think the answer to your problems is going to come from an ad on Facebook?"

"No ... wait. Here it is!" She thrust it under her sister's nose, which wrinkled instantaneously.

Then, much to Audrey's chagrin, Sabrina started to laugh.

Audrey pouted. "What? Are you looking at it? Look! A dollar, for a house in paradise. That's a total deal. I think it might be a sign."

Sabrina made a clicking sound with her tongue. "Aud. Are you serious?"

"Yes! Doesn't it sound amazing?" She clapped her hands.

"No. That's a scam. It's right up there with Nigerian Princes."

Audrey's hopes plummeted. She took the phone back and opened the link. "You think? I don't think so. It makes sense. They have all these old houses and they just need people to come in and rehabilitate them. To make them livable again."

"Yes, the key phrase is 'make them livable again,' meaning they're not livable now," Brina said, rolling her eyes. "And what do you know about restoring an old house? In a country that probably doesn't even have a Home Depot?"

"But Dad—"

"Dad did the work. We mostly just sat around while he was doing his contractor jobs, inhaling sawdust and paint fumes and asking when it was time for dinner." She held up a hand. "He also had a Home Depot."

Audrey gnawed on her lip. Brina could always be relied upon to deliver the truth bombs.

"Not to mention that you don't even know how to say hello in Italian."

"I do," she murmured, still staring at the phone, burning the image into her retinas. Of course, *ciao* was about all she knew how to say. Good thing it meant both hello and goodbye. How much harder could all the words in between be? "And I did learn a thing or two from Dad. Didn't you?"

Brina scrunched up her face. "Nope."

That was true. But Brina hadn't paid as much attention as Audrey had. Up until the time her dad up and moved out when she was twelve, Audrey was her dad's mini-me. Audrey had often followed her father around those massive Back Bay mansions he had the luck of restoring, asking to help. She'd learned a few things.

Of course, that was a long time ago.

"He walked out on us, remember?" Sabrina added. "I'm glad I didn't learn anything from him."

Audrey frowned. Brina had always taken the hard tack when it came to Miles Smart. *Good riddance,* she'd said, which was the way her mom felt, too. But Audrey had a soft spot for her dad. He had a wanderlust. Hadn't wanted to be tied down. Maybe there was more of him in her than in Brina.

Brina took the phone from her, slipping it back into her purse, and poured Audrey another glass of wine. "Besides, honey, that's just the *vino* talking. You know that you'd never do anything like that."

"What do you mean? Of course I would. I *could,*" she said, staring at her glass. Was it just the wine talking? No ... even though she was getting tipsy, it seemed like it was perfect. The answer to all her problems.

"It's all right not to be reckless. It's a good thing."

"This isn't reckless."

"Even if it isn't. Honey. Remember when you got that scholarship to UCLA?"

Audrey's eyes met her sister's. She knew where this was headed. "Yes, but I was only eightee—"

"You really wanted to go. You were ready to send in your paperwork. And then ... you bailed. Right?"

Audrey frowned. "But I—"

"Point is ...you are not a risk-taker. You've lived in Boston all your life. You'll die here," she said with a shrug. "And it's okay. You don't have to go anywhere. Everything you need is right here."

The wine was definitely starting to go to her head. When she closed her eyes, visions of warm sunshine, cool breezes, and a quaint little home on a cobblestone street, with flowers bursting out of window planters, crowded her mind.

Sure, she could probably find everything she needed here. Maybe not now, but eventually.

But what if she *wanted* something else?

CHAPTER FIVE

Audrey woke with the standard hangover three glasses of red wine normally gave her.

She was a lightweight, so she'd expected this. Hadn't cared much then. Didn't care much now. It'd been a necessary evil. It'd gotten her through the night.

Though, as she stared up at the water stain on the ceiling, her situation did not appear any rosier with the dawn of the new morn, like she'd hoped.

She moved her head only a fraction of an inch from the pillow before deciding that it would likely pop off if she attempted to move it any more. She groped around the bedside table for her phone, swiping it onto her chest and tapping the screen to wake it up. The brightness of the display scalded her tender retinas.

The first thing that came in sight when she regained focus was a picture of that Italian paradise. It wasn't hard to find this time, because apparently, in her half-drunken haze last night, she'd gone and made it her wallpaper. For both her Home screen *and* her Lock screen.

She had a foggy memory of the T-ride home, almost as if it'd happened decades ago. She vaguely recalled the smell of unwashed bodies, ripe from marinating in the day's heat at the Red Sox game, all packed into the train car like sardines. The wine had mellowed her. She hadn't even minded riding up against some drunken college kid's armpit. Now, the smell of it and the old alcohol lingered on her skin, making her want to retch.

Then her bleary eyes focused on the time.

Eight forty-five.

"Mother of pearl!" she shouted, rocketing up out of her bed. There were worse things than her head popping off. Namely, being super-late to her job and having the Dr. Brice Wattses and Dr. Emerson Ferrises of the world give her trouble.

She showered and readied herself in record time, boarding the T for a ride that was only slightly preferable to last night's, and only then, because she'd been three sheets to the wind. This time, she found herself sandwiched between a scowling, *I-hate-the-world* teenager whose Death Metal was so loud he might as well have not been wearing earbuds, and a man who smelled like salami. The combination of the two roiled her already queasy stomach.

To take her mind off it, she pulled out her phone and once again found herself transported to that charming cobblestone street under the bright sun. She sighed as usual, then pulled up the website and paged through the other photos. There were many of the town, each one more breathtaking than the next. Small outdoor cafes. An open-air market. A harbor dotted with tiny boats. A small, rustic stucco church with an old brass bell.

Underneath, it said, *READY TO OWN YOUR PIECE OF PARADISE?*

Yes, Audrey screamed in her head. She clicked the link to find photographs of young people standing in front of their purchases, looking as if they'd just won something big from Publisher's Clearinghouse. *That could totally be me.*

Then she read the paragraph underneath: *We'd love to welcome you to our happy town. If you'd like to own a piece of paradise, just enter the lottery for one of these properties listed below. Bid must be at least $1 USD, and buyer must agree to pay $1,000 deposit and make required repairs to the property at their own expense within one year of purchase. Winners will be notified by email. Good luck!*

She scrolled down a list of properties. Just addresses. She clicked on one that said "Piazza 3," and it brought up a photograph of what looked like a map of a housing development. There was a big circle and an arrow around one of the boxed-off sections.

She imagined it, right then, in perfect detail. Going out to her little wooden mailbox to grab a letter from her sister, smiling at the address. *To: Audrey Smart, Piazza 3, Sicily, IT.*

She tapped to see if there were more photographs, but no. Really? Would someone buy a home, sight unseen? It sounded risky.

Then she thought about what Brina had said to her. *You are not a risk-taker. You were born in Boston. You'll die here.*

Why did that sound so boring? She'd been happy with Boston up until a few years ago. But lately, something had been building inside her, and like a bottle of soda being shaken, the lid was about to come off. Explosively. All of her friends at the reunion last night had done things, gone places, had experiences. And what did she have? Did she want to live her life not having done absolutely anything?

"That's nice," a voice said beside her.

She looked up and realized Salami Guy was peering into her lap. She couldn't tell whether he was infatuated with Sicily, too, or if he was another creep who'd lean in and smell her hair. It didn't matter. The T was coming to her stop at the Back Bay station.

After one last glance at the almost-mythical land of Sicily, she decided it was nothing but a pipe-dream. A lottery? She'd probably never have the winning bid. And even if she did, would she be able to drop everything and fly there, alone? There were other, safer ways to *do something* with her life. Work at the food pantry. Write a novel. Send in thirty-three cents a day to spiritually adopt a child from a third-world country. She didn't have to go crazy.

She quickly extricated herself from between her two travel companions, pocketed her phone, and made a mad dash for Back Bay Animal Care.

*

Audrey yawned for the hundredth time that morning as she helped a little old lady out the door with her carrier. She lifted the hard-sided case up and peered at the hazel-eyed Persian. "You take care of your momma, okay, Pumpkin?"

As was typical, the cat gave Audrey an uninterested look, like, *No thanks.*

Audrey handed the carrier to the woman. "Here you go, Mrs. Heffelbower. Are you sure you can make it to wherever you're going?"

"Oh yes. I'm just a block down the road. Such a nice young lady," she said with a smile, patting Audrey's hand. "You should settle down. Marry one of those nice, competent doctors in there. Let them take care of you."

Audrey smiled. Pumpkin had been under her care since she started working at the animal clinic, but Mrs. Heffelbower still didn't seem to realize that Audrey herself was an actual doctor. Join the club. She'd already explained that twice today, and didn't feel like going into it again.

"Thank you," she said as the lady turned away. "I'll keep that in mind."

She went back inside and came face-to-face with Dr. Ferris. He frowned. "Smart."

"Ferris," she replied, matching his tone.

Of all the more experienced vets on staff, she liked Ferris least of all. Even less than Brice Watts, if one could believe it. He looked like a soap opera doctor, with his thick dark hair and piercing blue eyes, and he had quite a way with patients, which accounted for Mrs. Marx's

26

infatuation. But under those surface good looks and that winning bedside manner?

Dwelt a total, complete, and utter jerk.

Emerson Ferris was a lot like Brice Watts ego-wise, except worse, because instead of just thinking he looked like a movie star, Ferris actually *did* look like one. Thus, though all of the women in the practice fawned over him, none were actually good enough for him, not even for a tumble in his office, like Dr. Watts was rumored to be fond of. When he wasn't tending to his patients or schmoozing their owners, he stalked about with a major stick up his backside, criticizing everyone for existing. He had complaints that ranged from moving his Vitamin Water in the fridge to standing in his all-important way while he attempted to get from point A to point B in the hallway. Audrey had come around to calling him the Scarecrow. Behind his back, of course.

Oh, and another thing? As nice as he was to the patients? It was all a lie.

He hated animals. Their owners, too.

In fact, he really didn't like anything except himself. Whom he loved with a passion.

She attempted to scuttle past him, since she knew there'd be hell to pay if she wound up in his glorious way, but then she remembered Marx. She sighed. "Donut. In observation area six. Mrs. Marx wanted you to take a look at him. When you have time, of course."

His frown transformed to an annoyed scowl. "What's wrong with the little rat?"

"He imbibed alcohol."

"*Great*," he snapped, whirling on his heel and tossing a few choice curse words into the air. He checked his Apple Watch. "There goes my racquetball appointment. That Marx woman should be the one on a leash."

Well, at least she agreed with him there. "Sorry."

He paused for Audrey and motioned her ahead of him. "Lead the way, Doctor."

As if he didn't know where the observation room was. Audrey walked him down the hall, to area six. Donut was still in his kennel, looking much more alert. Better. She instinctively put out a hand, and he licked it.

Ferris looked at her. "Do you mind?"

She shook her head and stepped away, sticking her tongue out at him behind his broad back, and fully not caring how immature that made her.

Ferris set to taking the dog's vitals, just as she had done. Stethoscope in his ears, he murmured, "You pump his stomach?"

"No. We ran intravenous fluids, and he seemed to respond to the charc—"

He straightened and turned to her. Uh-oh. Wrong answer. "You're telling me you didn't pump his stomach?"

She shrugged lamely. "I didn't see the need of putting him through that. He seemed to be responding to—"

"The *need* was that this patient could've died," he snarled, his voice growing louder. "This particular breed and size is sensitive to even one drop of alcohol. Or didn't they teach you that in vet school?"

He should've known. He'd gotten his DVM from Tufts, same as she had, though he'd been a year ahead of her. *And* a pompous jerk, even then.

"You should know it's traumatizing to an animal to have to withstand that, especially a small animal like Donut."

He shook his head. "Death from alcohol poisoning would've been more traumatizing, don't you think, Audrey?" he said, his voice condescending. And since when did he ever use her first name?

Vet techs had come in to see what the commotion was. Now there was a little audience. Audrey's pulse pounded in her ears. She flipped her ponytail and crossed her arms. She didn't want to get into this, but if he was going to make her, then *fine*. "First of all, *Emerson*—"

"What's all this?"

They both whirled to see Dr. Carey, the medical director. The slight, gray-haired lady might have been small, but the woman packed a no-nonsense punch. Audrey had always admired the way she could cut through the other doctors' conflicting egos and defuse all kinds of employee disagreements. She was smart. Just. A dose of sorely needed perspective around here.

Good. Audrey smiled. She'd put the Scarecrow out in the field, where he belonged.

"Dr. Ferris and I were just having a disagreement about the proper treatment of this animal," she explained.

"No disagreement," Ferris said, glaring at her. "Dr. Smart clearly administered the wrong treatment, and she's trying to save face. This creature could've died."

Dr. Carey was already grabbing her stethoscope, her eyes trained on poor Donut. She listened to his heart, as meanwhile, behind her back, Audrey and Dr. Ferris regarded each other like competitors in a dogfight, each daring the other to deliver the first blow.

Dr. Carey removed her stethoscope from her ears and shook her head. "Well, that would be the standard treatment, though it appears the subject is doing much better, regardless. But I did receive a call from the owner."

Audrey's eyes snapped to the older vet's. "What? You mean Mrs. Marx?"

She nodded and pressed her lips together. Not just a call. Knowing Mrs. Marx, it was a complaint. "Yes. But—"

"And what, exactly, was it about?"

"Well, she was pretty insistent that the care of Donut be transferred exclusively to Dr. Ferris. I asked what it was that upset her, and she said that she felt slighted, and that her concerns were dismissed."

"Clearly dismissed," Ferris echoed. "The dog should've had its stomach pumped."

Audrey shook her head. "*She* felt slighted?" Audrey said in disbelief, her voice gradually rising. "You weren't there, Doctor. She dismissed me. Like everyone who seems to think I'm nothing but some kind of intern here. I have the same credentials as all of you and yet I'm treated like some lesser being just because of the way I look. I'm sick of having to explain myself twice to people! To the pet owners! To Watts! To Ferris!"

Meanwhile, Ferris grinned quietly, gloating. Smug jerk.

Dr. Carey took her by the arm. "Why don't we discuss this in my office?"

Audrey shook her head, now indignant. She no longer cared about the audience. This should've been a lesson to them, anyway, that they could do everything exactly right and save little pet lives and yet *still* get in hot water.

It. Wasn't. Fair.

She planted her feet. "No. What am I? In trouble? You're going to write me up? I did everything right! Just because Marx didn't like me, because I was young and a woman, doesn't mean I did anything--"

"Dr. Smart," the older vet said in a warning tone.

What, now they were going to say she was overreacting? Ferris continued to gloat, now chuckling at Audrey's situation. God, she hated him. She hated him, and Carey, and everything about this place.

"You know what? Forget it," she said, tearing her stethoscope off her neck, then ripping her nameplate from her coat. "You all treat me like a second-class citizen. I don't need this. I'm done. I quit."

CHAPTER SIX

Dr. Carey followed her out the door. "Are you sure you want to do this? Won't you reconsider, Dr. Smart? You're a valuable member of our team."

Audrey didn't even turn around. *Valuable, my butt.* She hoped that Dr. Carey would follow her into the T and attempt to lure her back with an extra big benefits package, but the second she reached the edge of the parking lot, Dr. Carey was gone.

It didn't matter.

Free! She was free!

The feeling was beyond invigorating. No big benefits package was worth that. She'd been so delighted by stupid Ferris's shocked expression (*guess you're going to be working overtime from now on, buddy, so you can kiss racquetball goodbye for the foreseeable future!*), so pumped by the way Dr. Carey practically begged her to come back, that she was a little drunk on the power. She felt almost immortal. The overwhelming urge gripped her to scale a mountain, bungee jump off the Lenny, eat the questionable sushi from that walk-up place on the corner, anything. *You say I'm not a risk-taker, Brina? Well, take that!*

The sun was bright and warm, something she never took time to appreciate because she was always buried under work in the clinic. The midday T was nearly empty. She had a car almost to herself, something she never knew was possible within the constraints of that soul-sucking day job.

Good riddance! she thought smugly.

Yes, that job had really sucked. That stupid apartment in Southie, too. No wonder she had nothing substantial to list among her world experiences. It'd all been holding her back, squelching her possibilities, holding a thumb down on her ability to go out and suck the marrow out of life.

No more.

On the train, she pulled out her phone and navigated to the website, which had become part of her favorites—SicilyParadise dot com. After a quick scan of the twenty or so offerings, finding no pictures of any of them, she went back to Piazza 3 and clicked on it. She read:

This house is located in Mussomeli, a city in the heart of Sicily, Italy.

In Mussomeli you will live the ancient Sicily, the real Sicily that you've always dreamed of. The city of Mussomeli is home to the Manfredi's Castle and traditions. It is a place of enduring beauty. If you buy a home in Sicily, you will not only have a house, but the opportunity to experience our culture, our timeless and treasured traditions, the slow and relaxed life of one of the most tranquil and safe lands in all the world.

Mussomeli is located in an inner hilly area, east of the Platani River, in Central Sicily, at 765 meters above sea level. It is 53 km from Agrigento, 58 km from Caltanissetta, 99 km from Enna, 199 km from Ragusa. The weather is continental, cool and dry in winter, warm and windy in the summer. There are few snowy episodes in winter. Street: Vicolo Piazza 3.

Amenities:
Air conditioning
Balcony
Canteen
Chimney
Electrical system
Furniture
Garage
Heating system
Lift
Parking within 100m
Reachable by car
Terrace
TV system
Views X

Sounded good. Really good. Peace? Tranquility? Safety? Yes, please. Plus, it had air conditioning, a television, furniture, an elevator. It wasn't just some hole in the ground. And it was only a dollar.

It was everything she wanted. Everything.

She clicked on the bright red BID NOW button, still thinking that she could back out if she really wanted to. But now, she didn't want to. She clicked on the application, which asked her various questions, the first being: *Why do you want to live in Sicily?*

Audrey didn't think. Her thumbs flew across the keyboard. She wrote: *As a veterinarian, I have dedicated my life to helping animals.*

Though I love the work, I have lived all my life in Boston, and decided that at this point in my life, I would like to experience a different part of the world. It has always been my dream to visit Italy, so I feel that now is the best time to do so.

She flirted with the box that said, *Please list your highest bid,* imagining a number that she wouldn't mind losing if she decided to back out. She didn't really *have* much money to lose. Plus, there was the matter of that $1,000 deposit. Finally, she typed in $1.

Then she auto-filled the requisite information, her address, phone number, credit card info. Before she could talk herself out of it, she jabbed the PLACE BID button. The screen buffered for a second, and then that lovely Italian photograph that had lured her in appeared, along with, *Congratulations! Your bid has been placed. You are one step closer to paradise!*

Satisfied, she pocketed her phone as the train pulled up at her stop.

It only really hit Audrey when she'd left the T station and was on her way to her apartment, a tiny cardboard box of all her work belongings tucked under her arm.

She was not just free.

She was also jobless. Almost penniless, except for the tiniest little robin's nest-egg in her 401k. Completely directionless.

And she'd just placed a bid on a home halfway across the world.

If that didn't scream reckless, she didn't know what did.

Doesn't matter. I didn't even get the house yet, she told herself, shrugging. Making plans to update her resume, she pulled out her phone and checked her email. An Old Navy ad, something saying her bank statement was now available, an Organizational Tip of the Day email her sister had signed her up for, a Cruises R Us promotion she'd opted into years ago.

Suddenly, her phone began to ring from a strange number. A really strange number. It said UNDISCLOSED, and it looked slightly … international?

Maybe it was someone in Sicily, confirming her bid. Likely. She answered. "Hello?"

"Yes. Audrey Smart?" a heavily accented voice said. Italian, definitely.

"Yes?"

"This is Maria Lombardo, a real estate agent in Mussomeli, Sicilia," she said so quickly, Audrey wasn't sure it was actually in English. "I received your bid?"

"Oh, yes. Thank you for confirming."

32

"Are you really a veterinarian?"

Great. It wasn't enough that she got doubt from the people she worked with; now she had to get it from halfway across the world. "Yes. Yes, I am."

"Will you be seeking employment as a veterinarian in Mussomeli?"

She frowned. She'd only quit her last job twenty minutes ago. She'd expected to marinate in her unemployed status a little longer than that. "Well, I suppose, eventually—"

"There is a shortage of skilled people like you here. The house is yours, if you want it."

Audrey froze in the center of the street, so that whoever was behind her nearly tripped into her. She stumbled over to a nearby streetlamp, holding onto it for support. "But—"

"We waive the deposit for skilled professionals who seek work in town. Si?"

She stared at nothing in particular on the sidewalk, now more convinced than ever that this was a scam. Or was there some catch? She'd submitted that bid not more than five minutes earlier. "Um ..."

"I email you my details. Call me with questions. And welcome, Audrey."

The call ended. Still clutching the streetlamp, Audrey's knees wobbled.

Her phone dinged with a new email. Her face flooded with heat and her fingers trembled as she clicked on it.

Congratulations! We are happy to welcome you to our beautiful little community of Mussomeli, Sicily! Please call our office at the below number to arrange for inspection and to complete the additional paperwork.

Audrey let out a little squeal, turned on her heel, and walked right back to the train station.

I own a house in Italy, she thought in disbelief. *I OWN A HOUSE IN FREAKING ITALY.*

*

Audrey still hadn't quite accepted it by the time she got to Beacon Hill.

She kept repeating it over and over in her head, until she got into a rhythm with every step she walked. *I OWN. A HOUSE. IN FREAK. ING IT. A LY.* As she walked, faster and faster, the words got faster and faster in her head until they all bled together as one.

Climbing up the stairs to her sister's brownstone, she rang the doorbell, still keeping the rhythm in her head.

Brina answered, Byron on her hip, a pair of chic reading glasses perched on the end of her pert nose, her iPad under her arm.

Before Brina could ask why Audrey was there at this time of the day, Audrey exploded like a time bomb. *"I OWN A HOUSE IN FREAKING ITALY!"*

Byron giggled gleefully. Brina's jaw dropped. "You what?"

"You heard me! *I OWN A HOUSE IN FREAKING—"*

Before she could finish, Brina grabbed her arm and yanked her into the house. "That's what I thought you said. Come in before the neighbors think you're going insane."

She might have been. Audrey wandered inside, still shell-shocked, then went back to the foyer and kicked off her shoes when she remembered Brina's rule.

"You seriously didn't. You mean that website?"

Audrey nodded. Byron smiled toothlessly at her in his blue sailboat onesie. She instinctively took him from Brina, balancing him on her own hip and doing the little rocking motion that he liked. "I did. I bid a buck. And then they emailed me immediately, saying my bid was accepted."

She leaned into his head to sniff his yummy six-month-old baby smell, and his wispy blond hair tickled her nose. Meanwhile, Brina stared at her. "Wait. What are you doing here in the middle of the day? Are you off from work today?"

Audrey was in the middle of lifting Bryon's body up so she could tickle his round belly with her nose, making him giggle maniacally. "Oh. I quit that."

"You what?" Brina's eyes bulged. "You did not. Today?"

Audrey nodded.

"Jeez, Aud. When I said you weren't reckless last night, I meant it as a compliment. Not something I wanted you to change."

Just then, the "twins" came running down the stairs. They weren't really twins; Macy was five and Delia was four, but the two of them were just as close as Audrey and Sabrina had always been. "Aunt Aud, Aunt Aud!" they cried, tackle-hugging her at the waist.

Macy jumped up and down like a bouncy ball and dragged her bottom lip down past her chin. "Look, I lost a tooth."

"Wow, neat!" she said, bending to give them kisses.

"Out!" Brina directed before she could. "Your aunt and I are talking! Adult time, remember? Remember what I said?"

The two little blonde girls nodded obediently.

She pointed up the stairs. "Good. Go play Barbies in your room."

Audrey managed to get a couple kisses in before they ran off, their little sock-covered feet making far too much noise for their little bodies on the wood staircase.

Brina rolled her eyes and motioned her toward their gorgeous eat-in kitchen, where she set a kettle to boil on the stove. "You were saying? About your job?"

"Oh. Well. You know. Ferris—"

"Ugh, is this about him?" she mumbled, standing on her tiptoes, grabbing two mugs from the top cabinet and setting them on the granite countertop, filling them with tea bags. "Ferris the Fart. What'd he do now?"

Apparently, Dr. Ferris had a number of nicknames, none of them incredibly mature. Reliably, Brina had met him at some veterinary school function Audrey had dragged her to, and said, "That guy's underwear must be really twisted in his pants. Stay away from him." Again, she'd been so right.

Audrey placed Byron in his swing, turned the dial so a tinkling version of Twinkle, Twinkle, Little Star played, and slipped onto a stool at the center island. She said, "Well, it doesn't matter anymore, does it? He was acting like the jerk that he is, I couldn't take it, so I quit."

"You walked out? Just like that?"

She nodded. "Carey begged me to come back. Well, not exactly begged. Asked hopefully. But my mind was made up." She lifted her phone. "So on the way home, I said, what the heck? And I placed the bid. It was accepted. On the spot."

"Really? Wow."

Audrey could usually read her sister's thoughts, but right now, she couldn't. Brina looked astonished, but also a little … worried? Probably with good reason. It was kind of out-there. "Anyway, I know you don't approve, but—"

"I never said that!" Brina said as the kettle began to whistle. She grabbed it and poured the tea. "I just said that I didn't know if it was the best idea for you. Because you know, you're—"

"I know. I'm a wuss. But I've been thinking about it. I need to make a change. I can't live like this for much longer," she mumbled, her shoulders slumped.

Brina looked at her, nodding her head sympathetically. "I get it. So, what does this place look like?"

35

Audrey bit her lip. "I don't know."

"You don't know?"

She pulled out her phone and scanned to the listing. She pushed it over to Brina, who read it. "Wow. Well, it sounds really nice. Nicer than I thought. It has air conditioning?"

Audrey looked at the listing and shrugged.

"Where is that? What is it called? Mussolini?"

"Mussomeli," Audrey corrected, entering the name on her maps app. It brought up a little place right in the very center of the island of Sicily. "Looks like it's in the mountains. Hmm. I wonder if you can see the water from there?"

Brina brought her mug of tea over and peered over her shoulder. "Well, it's an island. And I guess it'll be an adventure."

Audrey stared at her sister. Part of the reason she'd come all this way was because Brina was so good at talking her down from the ledge. "Aren't you going to tell me I'm crazy, wanting to uproot myself and fly halfway across the world?"

Brina shook her head and leaned her elbows on the counter. "Well. You *are*. But maybe you're right about this. You're in a rut, right? Maybe you need to shake things up a little. Maybe this is the universe telling you that." She paused. "And I always thought you should've gone away to UCLA. You're ready. Whether or not you know you are."

Audrey peered at the location on the map, in the middle of an island, in the middle of a sea, in the middle of the world, so far away. "You really think it's a sign?"

She smiled. "Yeah. Maybe. Besides, you can always come back if it doesn't work out. Boston'll still be here waiting for you." She sipped her tea. "And maybe you'll get to see if any of Dad's Mr. Fix-It tendencies rubbed off on you. Do you have any money saved?"

Audrey nodded. "Well. A little. I have a 401k. I can use that. And I can defer my student loans for a year. The real estate agent said they're waiving the deposit as long as I work there. I guess they have a veterinarian shortage."

"Wow." Brina grinned. "Then I think you should do it. What's the worst that can happen?"

On cue, Byron squealed loudly, almost as if in agreement.

Leaning over the counter, emotions tumbling about inside her, she opened the email and read the instructions again. Yes, she was really going to do this.

CHAPTER SEVEN

Audrey's skin practically danced with shivers as she boarded the British Airways flight. She hadn't been on a plane in forever, since a trip to Disney World when she was twelve.

Once Audrey made the decision to move to Sicily and got the ball rolling, everything happened so fast.

She gave up her apartment easily, put all her belongings in storage, and booked the flight, all in a matter of two weeks' time. She deferred her student loans and got her finances in order, sort of. There were only a few people who mattered enough to her to tell them about it—her mother, a couple of neighbors. In fact, the ease with which it was done, with which she extracted herself from the city she'd grown up in, only served to affirm that she'd made the right decision.

Now, everything she'd need in her life had been boiled down to a few suitcases.

As she walked down the aisle of the airplane, scanning the rows and seat letters, she realized her seat was in the aisle.

Lame.

She stopped at her row and loaded her carry-on into the overhead bin. The older businessman at the window was already leaning against it, half-asleep. A very large man sat in the seat between them.

Audrey leaned over the man's massive belly and tugged on the man's business suit. He stirred, confused.

"Pardon me. Would you mind switching seats with me? This is my first time to Sicily, and I ..."

The man rubbed his eyes and pulled his *Wall Street Journal* from the front pocket. "Not at all, dear."

She smiled. Another fortuitous thing. It was like everything was working out for good. She could feel it. Sure, the large man grumbled a little bit as he tried to remove his seatbelt, and then there was a bit of fumbling like a game of musical chairs, but then they all settled into their seats, and all was well.

Pulling off her jacket and adjusting the vent overhead, she said to the large man, "I'm sorry. I wanted the window seat so I could see the beautiful Italian countryside as we land! I know we have time, but I'm excited."

It was an eleven-hour flight to Palermo, with a stop in Heathrow, so it'd be miserable to have no one to talk to. At first, she thought he might not be much of a travel companion, but then he cleared his throat and said, in very accented English, "You don't travel much?"

She shook her head. "First time out of the country. I only had a passport just in case. I never used it before now. So, do you live in Sicily?"

She was aware she was chattering too much, and the plane hadn't even left the gate, but she couldn't help it. She always talked too much when she was nervous. Excited. Nervously excited.

"Yes. I live in Palermo. I visited my brother up in Portland. Are you visiting?"

"No. I bought a house, actually. In Mussomeli?"

His brow knit in confusion. "Why would you want to go there?"

That didn't sound good. In fact, he might as well have said, *Why would you want to go to that pit of utter despair and ruin?* "Do you know it?"

"Eh. A bit. It's inland. A young thing like you, going out there by yourself?" He inhaled sharply and she thought there was a little bit of dread in his voice, something he was reluctant to tell her. She shoved it off. "You buy from one of those—eh—website?"

She nodded, then took her phone off of Airplane Mode to show him the website. He looked at it quietly for a few seconds and said, "Well, *in bocca al lupo.*"

Audrey stared at him, head tilted. She'd expected him to say something like *Buona fortuna,* or something, which she thought meant "good luck." "What does that mean?" She grabbed her pocket dictionary. "I don't …"

He chuckled. "It means, in English, in the mouth of the wolf."

"Oh." Now she was more confused than ever. She had a mental image of herself as Little Red Riding Hood, putting herself in the clutches of the Big Bad Wolf. "Thanks. I think?"

He laughed some more and shook his head fiercely. "No, it's a ritual we have. Like your 'break a leg'?"

"Ohhhh," Audrey said, catching on.

"And to that, you would just say, *Crepi.*"

"*Crepi.*" She tried to pronounce it exactly as he had, but failed miserably. "Which means?"

"*Die the wolf.*"

"Oh. Makes perfect sense." She looked out the window as the plane began to speed up. She hadn't even noticed it taxiing on the runway. She took a long last look at Boston as they sped down the tarmac at Logan, wondering when she would see it again. "As you can tell, I know no Italian whatsoever. Except *ciao*. And ... *cannoli*."

He burst out laughing. "Those are the most important ones." He motioned with his hands. "Come now. That can't be all you know. What about *Piacere*?"

She wrinkled her nose.

"Piacere. Mi chiamo Gabriele. Come sta?"

She threw up her hands, nonplussed. "I told you, I have no idea—"

"I just introduced myself. *Mi chiamo Gabriele.*" He touched his chest. The buttons on his polo shirt were open, wiry hair and a few thick gold chains escaping from its confines. *"And you are?"*

"Oh!" Now she was getting it. She pointed to her own chest. "Audrey."

"Piacere, Audrey."

She said the unfamiliar word slowly, letting it roll off her lips. "Thank you."

"Grazie."

"Right. *Grazie.*" She watched his thick lips as the words easily left his mouth. "Ugh, I don't speak it very well."

"Mi dispiace, non parlo molto bene l'italiano."

She tried, her tongue getting hopelessly tangled as she attempted it on her own. She laughed, and he did, too.

Despite the long flight, the hours went by quickly. Audrey spent a good amount of the time talking to Gabriele, finding out more about what he knew about Palermo and the surrounding areas, and of course, learning Italian.

After a while, he said, "Now tell me, what brings a lovely young lady like yourself to leave a great city like Boston for the wilds of Sicily?"

She sighed.

She must've been exhausted, because she opened her mouth to tell him it was too sad a story to talk about, but suddenly, it all slipped from her mouth like water down a storm drain. She told him everything. About her job at the veterinary practice, finding the ad while riding the T, the disastrous high school reunion ... everything.

" ... And you see," she went on, waving to the flight attendant to come take away her coffee. She dropped it in the trash bag. "It was like everyone in high school had gone on without me. They all had wonderful lives, and what did I have? Absolutely nothing."

"What does it matter to you, what these people think? They are … how you say … nothing. Right? All that matters is what you think about yourself. Yes?"

"I guess. But I guess I just don't feel too highly about myself on my own. I had all these dreams, and I was too scared to pursue them." She took a deep breath. "And I decided that if I wanted to live an extraordinary life, you have to take extraordinary measures. Am I right?"

He nodded. "Yes. So you bought the house?"

She slapped the tray table with her fist. "I bought the house. And I'm committed to this. To building a life there. I mean, I'm in my thirties. I don't want to go into my forties having had no adventures whatsoever."

"I see. That makes sense. My brother moved to Portland, we all thought he was crazy. But he loves it there. Among our friends, we call him the Brave One. If there is something in his life he doesn't like, he changes it. Sometimes I wish I can be the same." He shrugged his fleshy shoulders. "But not me. I am stuck living in Palermo, all my life."

She smiled. "Well, you can come visit me in Mussomeli. Okay? I will fix the guest room up for you. If there even is a guest room." She scratched her head. "I'm not entirely sure on that. The listing was a little sketchy about the number of rooms."

He laughed. "It is a deal."

When the plane landed in Sicily, she sighed at the sight of the blue Mediterranean sea, dotted with sailboats. Waves lapped at the edges of white sand beaches. She could feel the warmth of the bright sun, even though it was early morning, even through the window. There wasn't a cloud in the sky. Everything looked happier in the sunlight. "It's beautiful," she gushed.

"Welcome to my home," Gabriele said.

When the plane finished taxiing and the Fasten Seatbelt sign dinged off, Gabriele held his hand out to her.

"È stato un piacere conoscerla, Gabriele," she said, her words only slightly stilted, proud of all she had learned.

"Likewise," he said as they shook hands and he helped bring her carry-on down from the overhead compartment. "And remember, Audrey, mi cara, quando finisce la partita il re ed il pedone finiscono nella stessa scatola."

"What does that mean?" she asked, slipping her bag's strap over her shoulder.

His heavily lidded dark eyes suddenly twinkled. "I hope you will learn that on your own."

CHAPTER EIGHT

When she stepped off the flight, Audrey paused and inhaled deeply. The scent of freedom.

Actually, she was still stuck in the airport, and the air here wasn't much different from that in Logan. But still. It felt cleaner. Freer.

She was trundled along with the other travelers, in the direction of the luggage return. When she reached the carousel, Gabriele waved at her and headed out the door. Apparently, he'd only brought a carry-on, or else she would've liked to nab him to ask how to hail a taxi in Italian, just in case.

But she could do this. Alone. She didn't need anyone else.

So assured of that was she that when her luggage popped out of the return, she scuttled to the carousel and waved off a young man's attempt to help her, lifting her heavy flowered suitcases on her own. "Got it!" she said with a grin. "But thanks!"

Taking one handle in each hand, she rolled them behind her, out the sliding glass doors. The sun was rising high on the island. Despite the heat, the impressive mountains in the distance took her breath away. Beyond the many pillars and the parking lot, she gasped at the sight of a large, snow-capped mountain, jutting toward the sky like the Paramount Pictures logo.

"Wow," she whispered, then almost forgot that now she could take those breaths of Italian air. She did, dragging it into her lungs. There was plenty of it—it was windy and warm, at least seventy degrees, despite the early morning. Though she could still taste the sea, slightly, like she did back home, it was cooler, and fresher, and ... better. *Boston, eat your heart out.*

Turned out, she didn't need Gabriele's help. She found the taxi stand by the symbols and got in line. As she did, she studied her Italian-English dictionary to get the phrasing exactly right. By the time she reached the front of the line, she thought she had it down.

The young taxi driver with the wayward dark hair and the button-down shirt, open to reveal a wife-beater, eyed her as she clumsily wheeled her bags toward him. Accidentally, one caught on the base of stanchion that formed the taxi line, and down went the whole thing with a clatter. "Whoops!" She attempted to lunge forward to save it, letting go of the handle of her case, but then the suitcase sprung back, hitting the traveler behind her in the groin. He let out an "oof."

"Sorry! I mean, *scuzi!*" she said, looking up at the taxi driver, who didn't seem all that willing to help her out. Even when she wheeled the luggage right up to him, he just kept staring at her, like *Americans.*

"Mussomeli?" She lifted her book and said, awkwardly, *"Per favore portami a questo indirizzo."*

She held up her phone with the address, clearly written.

He stared at it for one beat, his thick brow narrowing. Then he burst out laughing.

She laughed too, because Jovial Taxi Man was much better than Serial Killer Taxi Man. Maybe there was something else to that laugh, but she didn't really want to think of what it could be. Only then did he grab her suitcases, effortlessly, and throw them into the back of his cab. At least now they were on their way.

"All right. Here we go," she said proudly, mostly to herself, then turned back to the poor man whom she'd given a crotchful of her suitcase. "Sorry again!"

She ran off the curb, opened the door, and slid inside the back of the car. She peeked over the front seats and saw the man's license. Antonio Puglisi. Sounded like a famous painter. He had a rosary attached to his rearview mirror and a dog-eared picture of a couple of skinny kids at the beach taped to his dash.

Maybe he was a struggling artist, with dreams of creation, who'd taken up driving a cab to support his beloved family. How romantic. How *Italian*!

He got into the driver's side and lurched into traffic on a heavy foot. "So, Antonio," she said, now thinking about the way he'd laughed when she showed him the address. "Do you speak English?"

He peered into the rearview mirror with eyes that said, *Don't even start, woman,* and turned up his radio, where someone was crooning "My Way" in Italian.

She took that as a no. She peered at the photos from the website on her phone and sighed again. Gorgeous. Then she looked out the window. Here it was—that bright Italian sun, the impressive mountains, the dark sea stretching out to the horizon, meeting the equally blue sky. White crags stuck out from the water, and boats dotted the harbor. As they pulled away from the airport, she saw brightly colored terra cotta and stucco buildings with red tiled roofs.

She nearly pressed her nose against the glass, trying to take in all the sights of the city on the sea. She almost didn't want to stop to send Brina a text, but she'd promised she would, when she got in.

Eventually, though, they left the city proper and turned inland, and civilization fell away. They passed grassy fields and gently rolling hillsides, studded with cows and horses. Mussomeli was nearly two hours from Palermo, according to the maps on her phone, so she took a break from the view to type in, *I'm here. It's more beautiful than I even imagined.*

A few moments later, her phone dinged. *You realize it's 2AM here?*

Whoops, she'd forgotten about time zones. *Sorry!*

Her sister responded a second later. *It's okay, I was feeding Byron. Little bugger still won't sleep through the night. And I was thinking about you. Glad. You get to the house yet?*

She smiled. She'd kissed her sister and her nieces and nephew goodbye at their home just over fourteen hours ago, and she already missed them. She typed in: *No, on my way to Mussomeli now.*

He sister replied, *Send me pics! I can't wait!*

Audrey couldn't, either. She tapped her fingers on the armrest, then rolled down the window and let the warm air blow through her hair.

After about another hour of driving into the hills, she leaned over and said, "How much longer?"

The man simply looked over at her and shrugged. Then he pointed to a cluster of homes in the distance, perched on a hill, half-hidden by trees, and muttered, "Mussomeli."

She scrambled across the back seat of the car to get a closer look. "Mussomeli? That's it?"

He nodded, not nearly as enthused as she was. This time, she did press her nose against the glass. The place, mostly old, gray stone, rose from the hillside like a mountain itself, a collection of buildings that looked like some kind of medieval fortress.

"It's amazing," she breathed wistfully, before realizing she didn't have to dream about it. It was hers. She had a place here, in this town, an actual address. This was her home.

A slight feeling of dread overcame her. *This is my freaking home.* She tamped that down. Her hands shook in her lap, so she flattened them against her thighs as they got closer, rising up higher into the hills so that her ears felt full and started to pop.

Finally, he pulled to a stop at the side of the road and opened the door.

Audrey looked around. Other than a flat, barren area on the other side of the road that looked like someplace where they used to test atomic weapons, there was nothing around. Nothing, except for some very crumbly, steep old steps, cut into the hillside.

Maybe the guy needed to take a pee break?

She sat there for a moment, waiting, but then she peered in the rearview mirror as he opened the trunk. In the crack between the trunk's lid and the car, she saw a flash of flowered fabric from her suitcase, heard the thud as he threw them on the ground.

Pushing open the door, she scrambled out of the back of the cab and over to him, adjusting her comfortable travel shorts, which were really just glorified gym shorts. "I'm sorry. Why are we stopping?"

"Mussomeli," he said with a nod. Audrey was now convinced that might be the only word he knew.

"Yes, but I gave you an address. Piazza 3." She held up three fingers. "*Tre?* Yes?"

He nodded and pointed up the staircase. "*Si. Piazza Tre.*"

"Oh? This is it?" She let out a sigh of relief. Somewhere, just up those steps, was her destiny. "Cool."

She reached into her purse and pulled out her credit card, went back to the car, and swiped. When she came out, those steps suddenly looked a bit steeper.

She winced at her big bags. "You wouldn't happen to be able to help me …"

He stared at her, and for the first time, she had a feeling he knew *exactly* what she was saying. Because he simply laughed like she was the funniest comedian on earth, waved her away, jumped in his car, and sped off, tires squealing, leaving Audrey choking in his dust.

What the heck have I done?

She tamped that down again. No, this was not the time to be a Negative Nelly. She waved a hand in front of her and gauged the steps. From here, three flights. That was it. She could manage it.

Dragging the two cases to the foot of the stairs, she decided she wouldn't be able to get them both at once. So she hefted the first one, stair by stair, up to the first landing. By then, it had to be over eighty degrees, and the hot sun seemed a lot closer because she was pretty sure her nose was turning red. Her T-shirt clung to her frame with sweat.

Not a problem, she thought, jogging down to get the second case. She repeated the motion until she was on the first landing with both cases. She took a few deep breaths, resting as she gauged the next obstacle. *Just a little bit more.*

Unfortunately, when she got to the top of the third landing, she realized there were three more staircases waiting for her. By then, she would've killed a passing mountain-climber for a sip of water, and her nose was definitely starting to blister.

She had to stop and sit on the steps several times to reclaim her energy, so it took the better part of an hour. Meanwhile, cars passed by on the street below, and it occurred to her once or twice whether any of them were looking at her like the idiot American who'd decided to scale a mountain with suitcases instead of a backpack. But she refused to let those thoughts intrude. *This is going to be good. This is going to be awesome. Just over this hill is everything I ever dreamed of.*

When she finally crested the last staircase, she looked around, breathing hard, searching out her home, her lovely Piazza 3.

But there was nothing.

No buildings. Nothing that even looked like an abode, not even a freaking hut. Just another hill and a gravel service road, stretching upward before winding around another hill. Beside that? A high, closed chain-link fence.

Her hands clenched into fists.

You're no artist, Antonio Puglisi, she thought darkly. *You, my friend, are a total jerk.*

*

About two hours later, after Audrey had gone up and down the hillside like a roaming mountain goat, but far less gracefully, she finally entered the city proper. She almost got down on her knees and kissed the asphalt, because it was far easier to roll her suitcases on it than on the gravel that had constantly been getting stuck in the wheels.

The place was, in a word, *adorable.* Just as those photographs had promised. She stepped past an old church with the rusty bell atop the door and a statue of the Blessed Mother outside, arms outstretched. She took that as a Welcome sign and headed to an open town square with a small stone fountain, a trickle of water dribbling between a grape-toting woman's breasts. Some of the buildings were quite modern, and a few cars were parked on the streets. It was the perfect combination of modern convenience and old-world charm.

She stopped the first person she saw, a woman on a bicycle with a basket, and, out of breath and too tired to grab her dictionary, said, "Please tell me you speak English?"

The woman nodded. "American?"

Audrey wanted to kiss the middle-aged woman with the fiery red hair, invite her into her house, if ever she could find it, for tea. But for now, she just nodded. "I'm looking for a house."

"You are not the first American to be doing so," she said in a heavy accent. "Our city's been—how do you say?—flooded by foreigners lately. You have bought a one-euro house?"

Audrey nodded. "Well, one dollar."

"Ah." She peered at the address on Audrey's phone and smiled. "You're in luck. Your house is right down that road. Not far. Keep going until you see *Tre*."

"Oh. Thank you!" Audrey gushed, peering down the narrow street. It was old and quaint, with cobblestones, slanting down and curving out of sight. The homes were all collected together, sharing walls. Some were in better condition from the outside than others, others had small balconies. A clothesline hung across the narrow expanse, covered with someone's laundry. Birds perched on modern streetlamps, peering down at her.

"Good luck to you," the woman said, before pedaling off.

"Crepi," Audrey mumbled under her breath, staring down the street.

Fisting her hand around each of her big cases, she dragged them on the street. The lane was barely wide enough for her to pass through comfortably with both bags trailing behind her, without catching them on the front stoops of the homes. The cobblestone street slanted a bit to the center, in a V, with a thin rivulet of water draining downhill. She didn't pass a single person as she walked, so she peered in doorways as she counted the numbers down to *tre*. People had terra cotta potted plants and geraniums in their doorways, a couple of balconies on the homes were adorned with intricate scrollwork, and there were a few full milk bottles on a couple of the stoops.

So cute! They actually still have milk delivery?

Starting at 97, the numbers kept going down until finally, she spied number three down the hill, a gray, nondescript square. It was on the very corner, which as she remembered from the map, vaguely made sense. She let go of her suitcases and scooted up to it, standing before the front door.

Honey, I'm home!

Okay, well … it was old, but there was a definite charm to it. The gray, smooth river stone walls were crumbling, nearly eaten up by ivy. The rustic front wooden-plank door was full of holes and pits, and seemed to be lingering tentatively in the doorway like an unwanted houseguest.

But it was hers. The stoop, the rotting old door, the property, the walls, the whole darn address. All of it. Hers. And it was so cute. The windows had little shutters, and just like in her fantasy, there was a cute mailbox affixed to the doorway, for all those letters she'd be getting from Brina. With the right fixes, maybe a nice coat of paint, it'd be a postcard of its own. She could send it off to Brina in reply, make everyone at home wish they'd invested in Sicilian real estate, too.

She clapped her hands excitedly. She'd never owned a piece of real estate before. Because it wasn't hers, she'd been afraid to so much as nail a picture to the wall of her apartment in Southie. She could do whatever she wanted to this place; if she wanted to paint it bright pink, that was her prerogative. She'd been psyching herself up for this for the past two weeks, and was ready to put in the work, get her hands dirty, make it a home. *It's perfect.*

As if on cue, a stiff wind blew down the corridor, stirring up the clothing overhead and sending her hair flying in her face. An aluminum can skittered loudly on the stones, toward her. She watched it, until she heard an even louder, ungodly creaking noise coming from the direction of her new home.

And the front door suddenly collapsed to the ground with a terrific bang, two inches from her toes.

CHAPTER NINE

Is this the right place?

That question had been launched into Audrey's head the second the door fell at her feet, but only seemed to grow as she stepped inside.

She climbed over the refuse, into the front "foyer," if it could be called that. It was the size of a telephone booth. A second later, she ducked her head out and checked the number. 3. Yep. This was the right place. Across the way stood 2, looking remarkably more put-together.

Audrey slipped back in. A step through the entryway, she found herself in the kitchen, if it could be called *that*. The walls and floor were all crumbling plaster. It looked like the wreckage from a war-torn place, covered in dust and refuse. It smelled like mold and fresh dog poop. It had a wash basin, a table, something that might've been used as stove in some other century, and a massive hole in the ceiling. A skylight?

There were no windows in the room, so Audrey instinctively went for the light switch. She couldn't find one.

Wait, didn't they say this place had electricity? she thought, rifling through her purse for the informational brochure, which the agent, Maria, had sent her. She unfolded it carefully.

Sure enough, the paper definitely listed electricity, air conditioning, balcony, furniture, television … lift.

Something told her she wasn't going to find air conditioning or an elevator here. She'd be lucky to find working plumbing.

That was when she spotted an open doorway across the miniature kitchen. She climbed up a step, choking on the dust, and went across to it.

She grabbed her chest to keep from retching. Though it smelled like a bathroom, it had neither a toilet nor a sink. Just another hole, this one in the ground.

Staggering back, she grabbed her phone and pressed in a call to Maria. Maria answered after a few rings, spouting something in Italian Audrey still couldn't understand, even though she'd heard it about a thousand times in the last two weeks, every time she called to iron out a

49

detail of her plan. "Hi, Maria. It's Audrey. I'm here, in Mussomeli. At the property."

"Ah. Good. We'll have to arrange to come by. Lots of paperwork."

Audrey backed away from the offensive bathroom, *if it could be called that,* and went back into the foyer, which she'd already decided didn't deserve to be called that, considering it was smaller than a telephone booth. "Yeah ... um. About that. I was expecting it to be in a little better condition."

"Oh, well. It's a dollar," she reminded Audrey. She got the feeling that Maria had had this conversation before. "But it's two hundred years old, rich in history, and ... did you notice the view?"

"No, but—" There was a strange staircase, hooking off to the right. Strange, because she'd have to climb up almost waist-high to get to it. She stuck her head in, but all she could see was another wall up ahead, in terrible disrepair, and possibly another room. "One second."

Cradling the phone between her cheek and her shoulder, she hoisted herself up onto her backside and climbed to her knees, taking a fresh coat of chalky plaster with her. Brushing it off her, she climbed the tiny stairs.

"You see, it's nice. The town is really cute. But the house ... I thought it had things. Like air conditioning?"

Maria burst out laughing. "That place? Oh, no. No no. No. Not ever."

"The listing did say that it had it, though."

"It did?" There was a pause and the faraway tapping on a keyboard. "No. It doesn't."

Audrey climbed the steep stone steps, hugging the walls, which wasn't hard, because her shoulders nearly brushed both of them, the stairwell was so narrow. It was also better suited to someone who was about four feet tall, because she found herself crouching to avoid scraping the water-stained roof with her forehead. "Maria," she said. "I have the listing right here. And it says—"

"Well, all of the listings *say* those things. But unless there is an X by the amenity, the property does not have that particular amenity."

Audrey stopped on the step, squinting in the darkness at the page. She went down the list. There was only one X. For *Views.*

Oh, god. I am so stupid. "Ah, pardon me. I see now," she said sheepishly. "My mistake."

A pause. "I hope you're not reconsidering?"

Audrey frowned. Heck no, what did this lady think she was? It'd take a lot more than that to send her home with her tail between her legs. She was her father's daughter. She never backed down from a challenge. Besides, construction was in her blood. Well, sort of. "Of course not. Do you think you can come around this afternoon with those papers?"

"Certainly. Two?" Maria said, as Audrey rounded the corner into the bedroom. *If it could be called that.* It was tiny, full of garbage, and a yellow-stained mattress that had no discernable shape whatsoever.

She took two steps and then nearly went straight through the hole in the floor, to the pseudo-kitchen. "Yes. Two would be lovely."

She stepped over the hole and went to the window, drawing back ancient wooden shutters to the outdoors.

As she did, a gray blur flew in her face, letting out a wobbly sort of shriek.

"Ahhhh!" she screamed, dropping her phone and flailing her arms to get it away. What was it, some weird Italian ghoul? The spirits of the previous owners, trapped inside?

The thing flopped to the ground and righted itself as Audrey shoved her body away from the window, backing up so that suddenly she found herself treading on air for a mere split second before she began to sink.

Slipping one leg into the hole, right up to her knee, she realized it was only a pigeon as it hopped, unruffled, onto the windowsill. It looked back at her for the briefest of moments, like, *Aren't you a spaz?* and flew off, past its little corner nest.

She let out a sigh of relief, catching her breath.

"Miss Smart? Are you all right?" Maria's voice came from the phone on the floor.

From her trapped position, Audrey reached across the floorboards for it. Not quite tall enough. Pushing down on the floor, she managed to extricate her leg from the hole and grab the phone. "Just great. Are pigeons … dangerous around here?"

"*Scuzi?*"

There was no balcony, but it looked like there could be one, if she wanted to put one there. A cool breeze carried the scent of the ocean, citrus, and sweet basil. And it overlooked the most gorgeous, hilly vista, all the roofs of the buildings rising up to her, the trees below her, and in the very far distance, the ocean.

The advertisement was right. This was some view.

"Forget it. Do you know of any hardware stores in the area?" she asked.

Maria said, "I'll email you right now the addresses of some places that can help you."

"Thank you." She ended the call with Maria and rubbed her hands together. "This will work," she murmured, thinking of her father.

Miles Smart, her dad, had been one of the area's best contractors, a pro at flipping houses. He'd taken her and Brina off on a lot of his jobs, growing up. Though he mostly told them to stay out of trouble so they wouldn't get nails in their feet, she'd learned a little something from him. How to use a nail gun. How to handle basic repairs. She knew her way around a hammer. Plumbing. Electricity. She didn't know a lot, but she certainly had more experience than most women.

She'd be absolutely fine. *I'd be better if he was here, too.*

But no ... she'd pledged to do this herself. No help needed. And she would. She opened up her phone and started to jot down in the notes a list of things she needed to buy in order to get started. By then, Maria's email of the nearest hardware store had arrived.

She wheeled her bags into the front foyer, propped the door back in place as best she could, and headed out blindly, trying to find the store.

She'd fix this place into the best little house on Piazza ... even if it killed her.

CHAPTER TEN

Audrey trekked down the cross street that intersected with Piazza, following the map on her phone. As she did, she said *Ciao!* to just about everyone she came across, because she couldn't remember a single thing that Gabriele had taught her on the plane. Not that there were many people—the town was largely empty. The people she did run across, though, all smiled at her, and occasionally they'd say more, but Audrey just waved and continued up the street, hoping she wouldn't give away her utter cluelessness.

The lady she'd met when she first set foot in the city proper had said the village had been flooded with foreigners, but not a single person Audrey ran into seemed as out of place as she felt. They all seemed like very comfortable fixtures of Mussomeli, like they'd lived here their whole lives.

Maybe they are foreigners, but they'd easily adapted to life here. Maybe that will be me in a year. Maybe I will be totally Sicilian by the time I go back home. Maybe I won't go home at all. Maybe I'll only jet back for a quick visit, but have to leave because I miss Sicily too much. Maybe this will be my home.

The mix of old and new was truly a work of art, creating a unique look. The medieval architecture of some of the buildings was exquisite, with Baroque style, gothic features, Corinthian columns and wrought iron. Grotesque gargoyle ornaments peered down at her from both sides of the street, shaded by blooming olive trees. Between the buildings, she glimpsed a gorgeous view of the countryside, studded with green fields and mountains. In the distance, on one of the peaks, stood an impressive castle, melding into its rocky façade, like something out of a fairy tale.

She tripped over a pile of rubble on her walk, and realized it was a house that had just given up. It was one of many. The old homes were *very* old, some in danger of crumbling into the mountainside, and many of them looked abandoned, their open doorways like the mouths of dark caves.

There were a lot of shuttered businesses, too. She stepped past storefronts, peering beyond the dusty glass to see if any of them sold anything resembling hardware. There was an old vacuum store, and a store that sold nothing but religious figures. A butcher shop, with strings of sausage hanging in the window. A market with crates of onions and apples outside. All of this, she filed away for later.

There were only a few cars in this area, since most of the roads were too narrow. People zoomed by on bicycles. One brave soul slipped past her on roller skates, suicide considering all the broken cobblestones. Everyone seemed so fit and happy, too. No suited businessmen, heads down, frantic to get to their next meeting. The air smelled like basil and freshly washed laundry. It was all so cute. So homey. So welcoming.

Luckily, the hardware store wasn't too far away. Just two blocks south, past a road that had modern buildings mixed with rustic homes like her own, she found the double doors wide open, letting in the breeze. It had barrels outside, filled with rakes and shovels, and a couple of charcoal grills, and an old-fashioned, human-powered lawnmower. She stepped over the cracks in the curb and went inside, having a feeling that in the next few weeks, she'd probably become its best customer.

Knowing that, she smiled even bigger at everyone inside, so much that her face hurt. They probably thought she was insane. Especially at the man stocking the shelves and the woman behind the paint-mixing counter. But she wanted to be their best friends. Desperately. That was what her dad had taught her: *Rule number one in any renovation: Make nice with the folks at the nearest hardware store.*

Cleaning supplies, she told herself, reaching into her travel shorts for her phone so she could look at the list she'd typed in. *Bucket. Mop. Sponges. Cleaning solution. Hammer, screwdriver, wrench, drill, screws, and a couple of hinges for the front door.*

That would be a start. And, she realized, pretty much all she'd be able to lug with her, on her own.

The aisles were impossibly narrow and cluttered with assorted wares. The signs at the head of each aisle may have been a help, if she could've read what they said. After navigating up and down the aisles about a hundred times, she collected most of the items in a big red bucket, stuffed the mop and broom under her arm, and carefully found her way to the front of the store.

When she got to the front, the paint-counter woman was leaning against the register, looking bored. There was a red barrette atop her head, hopelessly lost in a tangle of black, wayward hair, and she had a bit of a long, pointed nose that made her look like the Wicked Witch of the West, minus the green skin.

Audrey approached the counter and said, *"Ciao!"* just as she heard a deafening crash behind her.

She whirled around, realizing she'd upended a dog tag display. Reaching down to pick them up, she knocked over a couple of bottles of spray paint from a shelf with the long, unwieldy mop and broom handles. Then she whirled back, narrowly missing a man in a greasy white T-shirt, who ducked just in time.

"Whoops! Sorry," she said as the cashier spouted Italian to her at a breakneck pace, motioning wildly at her. Finally, she tilted the offending mop and broom so they were upright and leaned them against the counter. "I mean, *scuzi."*

The woman gave her a disgusted look. "American?"

"Yes ..." Audrey admitted, withering under her stare. She pointed to the goods as the woman rang them up on the old-fashioned register. "Do you happen to deliver?"

The woman surveyed her things, and her eyes narrowed.

"Not this stuff, obviously. Obviously I can carry this myself. I'm just thinking, for the future. When I come back?" She tittered nervously, thinking of that bathroom, *if it could be called that.* "I'm fixing up a home around the block, and I'm going to need quite a bit of stuff. Including a toilet. Can you deliver a toilet?"

The woman looked blankly up from the price tag on the hammer and didn't say a word.

"Annnnd obviously I'm wasting my breath because you don't speak English," Audrey said with a sigh.

As the woman finished, Audrey reached into her purse and pulled out her wallet. She found her credit card in the sleeve and was just about to thrust it across the counter when the woman pointed to a faded, peeling sign, half-hidden underneath a display of lanyards and carabiners. It said, *No carta di credito.*

She didn't need to know Italian to know what that said.

"Oh, then ..." She picked through her wallet, finding a few American twenties. "You don't take—"

"No." She rolled her eyes.

"Um ..." She hesitated, fidgeting. "I don't have anything else. You see, I forgot to change out for euros. I thought I could just use a card everywhere."

The woman stared at her. "No."

I could use a little more help than that, she thought, sticking her card back in her wallet.

As if reading her mind, the woman touched her card and pointed outside, then started rattling off something in Italian that made Audrey's head spin. She listened, following her pointed finger, but it didn't make sense until she thrust a finger at the card and mimed putting it into a machine.

"Oh, an ATM? I can get euros from there?"

The cashier, obviously done, just crossed her arms. A couple of other people waited in line behind her. They didn't tap their feet or let out exasperated sighs, as Americans would have, but she still felt their eyes boring into the back of her head.

"Where did you say the ATM was?"

More Italian. Funny, when she'd set out for Italy, the Italian language had seemed so pretty, so melodic, she could understand why it was known as a romantic language. Now, it gave her a headache.

"One moment." She pointed to her things and backed toward the door, stopping abruptly when she came in contact with a rack of home improvement magazines. "I'll run and get cash. Just ... hold these right here for me? Please?"

Audrey dashed outside and stumbled about blindly for a bit, until she found a bank, and the ATM machine. Of course, there was a line. Waiting behind an old man, feeling the seconds tick by as the sweat trickled down her ribcage, dread pooled in her gut. *What are you doing, Audrey? If this disaster didn't tell you that you've made the biggest mistake of your life, what will?*

Finally, it was her turn. She nearly dropped to her knees in thanks when she saw a selection on the screen that listed a number of languages, including *English*. After a minute or two, she was able to extract two hundred euros, though she wasn't sure on the transfer rate. She hadn't looked at the total on the register and hoped that'd be enough.

She flew back down the street and exploded through the doors, but when she got back, it was like the moment had been frozen in time. The cashier was still there, in almost the same position she'd been before, as was the rest of the line, just patiently waiting for her return. A couple of the people behind her even smiled benevolently. In America, a stock clerk would've put her stuff back on the shelf by now and someone would have already keyed her car in the parking lot.

But you're not in America anymore, remember, Aud?

"Thank you for waiting," she said to them, opening her palm and pulling out the crumpled bill, which she flattened on the counter.

The lady at the register made change, handing her a few coins and bills. Thanking her, she pocketed the change and collected her purchases. The other people in line swerved out of her way, giving her a wide berth so she wouldn't smack them in the face with the broomstick.

"*Signorina,*" the lady behind the register said as Audrey turned to leave. She said it two more times before Audrey realized she was talking to her.

"Yes. Um, Doctor, actually."

"Delivery is free within the village limits," she said, in perfect English.

Audrey sighed. *"Grazie,"* she mumbled, then thought, *I think.*

So much for making best friends with the owner of the nearest hardware store. She wasn't sure she ever wanted to show her face there again.

CHAPTER ELEVEN

"Success!" Audrey cried as she finished screwing the hinge to the door frame.

It'd been tough to wrangle the heavy door into place, but somehow, she'd managed to prop it up there long enough to drill the brand new hinges into place so she could have a fully functioning door. When she finished, she spent the next few minutes just opening and closing the door, inspecting her handiwork. It was a darn fine door, if a little rustic, but that was great. It fit with the house. It was sturdy. They didn't make 'em like this anymore.

Just look at me now, Dad, she thought, smiling.

Well, one thing down, a thousand more to go, but at least she'd made her place safe from whatever intruders might lie in wait, in this town.

She took a couple of steps away from the stoop and held out her hands, fingers in a goalpost with the tips of her thumbs together, making a frame. Yes. It was all coming together.

Just then, a boy with a squeaky-wheeled cart came up the street and stopped in front of her. In his faded Pink Floyd T-shirt, jeans, and shaggy haircut, he could've passed for an American high schooler, circa 1970. Audrey smiled at him.

He smiled back. "Audrey Smart?" he said, in remarkably unaccented English.

"How did you know my name?" she asked, astonished.

He reached onto the cart and lifted up a Vera Bradley purse in a very familiar paisley pattern. Familiar, because it was hers. Which prompted her to ask the pressing question … when had she seen it last?

Also, did this mean he'd been going through it? Well, of course, he had to, in order to know her name, but still, she felt a little weird about strangers going through her things. "Where did you find it?"

He pointed down the street. "You left it down at my parents' store. You forget?"

"Oh!" The news didn't shock her. She'd gone running to get the money, and then she'd been so discombobulated, it wasn't a surprise she'd left it there. What did surprise her was that someone was bringing it back to her, and in relatively the same condition as it was before. She opened it; her credit cards and all the twenties were still there. Not that they'd do anyone good in Mussomeli. "Thank you. How did you know where I lived?"

He reached into the opening of her bag and pointed out the informational brochure from Maria, with the address of her new house, circled in red.

"Oh. Right. Well, I appreciate you delivering it to me."

The good-looking boy with the dark brown eyes smiled mischievously. "I have something else for you." He went around the side of the cart and pulled a burlap sack off a toilet. "My mama said you wanted one of these. We had this one out back. She thought you could use it."

"She did?" Maybe she'd misjudged the woman. Audrey patted her heart, touched. It was the first time a toilet had sparked that kind of reaction in her. "It's amazing. Thank you. How much do I owe for it?"

He shook his head. "It's free. Consider it a ... housewarming gift." He motioned to it. "Get the door and I'll bring it in for you?"

She scurried to the door and held it open as the boy hefted it into his arms and brought it inside the house. She motioned him through the kitchen, and he set the toilet down outside the bathroom and looked around.

"I think you have your work cut out for you," he said, whistling as he caught sight of the hole in the ceiling.

"It's okay. I'm fully prepared and ready to work," she assured him, looking around. "I'd offer you something to eat or drink but I actually don't have anything now, for obvious reasons."

He laughed. "That is all right. I am fine." He reached out a hand. "I did not introduce myself. I am Luca."

She shook it. "Audrey. But obviously you know that. How do you speak English so well?"

"Because I went to America for school. Two years. Free ride. I play your soccer there. But then I got hurt, and no more scholarship. They send me back." He shrugged. "I hope Mama wasn't bad to you. She hates Americans."

Now it was making sense why she'd receive a toilet as a housewarming gift. Well, it was better than nothing. "Oh, wow. I'm sorry."

He laughed. "It's okay. Now I get to live my dream of delivering toilets to pretty American ladies like you." He winked.

Audrey stiffened. What a Latin lover. Did he often deliver toilets to American ladies? And if that was the start of a flirt, she needed to shut that down fast. She may have looked around his age, but she had to have been at least ten years his senior. Plus, the last thing she needed was to think about dating. She had work to do. "I appreciate it."

He wiped his hands on his jeans. "You need help?"

"You would?"

"Sure."

She needed all the help she could get, especially since she really didn't have a huge amount of know-how when it came to plumbing. Plus, she hadn't actually used the bathroom since the airport, and she would have to soon. It probably beat asking a neighbor, or trying to find a public one. "All right. Great."

Luca pushed his shaggy long hair out of his face and inspected the set-up.

"I've been checking, and it looks like there's plumbing hooked up, and the supply line looks pretty decent," she said as he did. "But I probably need some bolts for the flange and caulk that I don't have."

He sat back on his haunches and jumped to standing. "That's why you have me." He pointed at himself with both thumbs.

He disappeared, and came back a second later with a toolbox. Together, they assembled the toilet, placed it solidly on the flange, and connected the supply line. It took fewer than thirty minutes, and then they were done. She twisted the valve to the "on" position and waited for the water to fill the tank. When it started to, she smiled. Yes, it was a little brownish, but that was to be expected. It actually wasn't too bad.

She stood up and rubbed her hands together. "Now, the test."

Bracing herself, she pushed the handle for the flusher, half-expecting water to fountain in her face like a bidet. But the water formed a neat little whirlpool and made a *glug glug glug* sound as it exited the bowl. That was a good sound, her dad used to say, a healthy sound. Then it slowly began to refill with newer, slightly less brown water.

"Yay!" she shouted, pumping her fist and giving Luca a high five. "Thanks. Couldn't have done it without you."

He waved that away. "My pleasure."

"Come back tomorrow and I'll let you install my sink," she joked, seeing him to the door.

He laughed. "Good luck. I am sure I will see you around the store, yes?"

"Probably so often, you'll be getting sick of me."

He paused in the doorway. "You're not actually staying here tonight? You stay in a hotel?"

She shook her head. "This is my home. I'll be fine here."

"Brave American lady." He winked. "Good luck."

When he left, Audrey spent more time just basking in the beauty of her toilet. Maybe it was foolhardy to think she could stay here while the renovations were being complete, but that was what made it an adventure. Plus, she didn't really have the cash to spring on alternative living arrangements.

She used the toilet, and not having a sink to wash up at, or toilet paper, for that matter, found some wet wipes in her purse. Then she flushed, twice, mostly to hear the sweet, musical, *glug glug glug.*

This time, it was more like a *glug glug gllllllaaaaaarrrrrggggg.*

The walls trembled. Was this an earthquake? Pompeii, the Sequel? An inhuman moan seemed to be coming from the pipes, all around her.

She whirled to the pipes behind her, where the sink should be attached, and some strange, gooey, black molasses-like substance began to slide out slowly, landing with a plop on the ground. Grimacing, she looked over at the shower stall, tucked in the corner behind a mildewed white curtain. A low, menacing wail emanated from deep within.

She fastened her hand around the curtain and, taking a deep breath, threw it back fast, like ripping off a Band-Aid.

Similar black goo was falling from the shower faucet, collecting in the drain like a living, breathing creature. Then there must've been an air bubble, because suddenly, the faucet spewed. Like vomit. A black, warm fist of goo slammed right into her chest, splattering there with an awful squelching sound.

She screamed.

Scarred for life, she ran out into the kitchen, wishing there was a door to the bathroom, because she would very much have liked to slam it, and keep it closed, possibly for the rest of … forever.

Instead, she went outside and stopped at her front stoop, where she gasped for air. She looked down at her ruined T-shirt and sighed as the stuff dribbled down her shirt. She touched it, and it trembled, like a frightened slug. It also smelled like garbage marinating in poop.

At least she had plenty of clothes to change into. She'd simply change her T-shirt. Not that she wanted to go back in the house just yet. Or … ever.

Tears threatened to well in her eyes, but she held them back. *You know what you need, Aud? A time out.*

CHAPTER TWELVE

After Audrey finally summoned up the nerve to go inside and change her T-shirt, she decided to go in the opposite direction from the hardware store, in search of someplace to eat lunch.

She followed her phone's directions to a café called *La Mela Verde*, still calling *Ciao* to the people she passed, though not as happily as before. She couldn't stop wondering if she'd get home and find her adorable little home transformed into a big black blob. Now her brand new housewarming gift was probably covered in it. She wasn't sure she'd ever be able to use it again.

It's perfectly fine, Aud. It was just a reaction to the flushing. The pipes are old and just need to be flushed out. You'll be able to go back there and get a plumber and it'll all be sorted out. It's fine.

When she arrived at the place on her map, she looked up and smiled.

It was the exact same café she'd seen in the pictures, with a bright yellow canopy, picket fence, and baskets of fruit in the windows. A few very Sicilian people were sitting at the umbrella-topped wrought iron tables outside, sipping their espressos and enjoying the beautiful weather.

She smiled and went inside, determined to fill her growling stomach with something she could buy with the rest of her euros. As soon as she stepped through the front door, her eyes fell on a green-eyed cat with patchy gray hair. As grungy as it looked, it still sidled up to her like the queen of its domain and curled its tail around her calf, begging to be petted.

Audrey'd never met an animal she could resist petting, so she crouched and stroked behind the little cat's ears, ignoring the many conversations going on around her in Italian, since she couldn't understand them anyway. But there were other languages, too. German. Spanish. Chinese. A few she couldn't make out.

"Oh, aren't you a pretty kitty," she said as she stooped in the doorway, in her standard baby voice that she only used with animals. At least animals only had one language. They just wanted to be loved.

"She likes you," a voice behind the counter said.

Audrey followed the sound to a muscular man in an apron and a skull cap. Simply too good-looking. Audrey already knew she'd never be able to have a normal conversation with him without giggling like a goofball. He had a number of tattoos up and down his biceps, but despite the rather rough appearance, his face bore a gentle smile, and his piercing blue eyes danced. "Um. Is she yours?"

"Clio? Nah. She belongs to the streets. Like most of the cats around here. Most are shy, but Clio isn't. She comes right in here and asks for her lunch."

Clio quickly lost interest in Audrey and scampered out the door. Audrey went to the counter, trying not to do anything stupid, which she had a tendency to do in the presence of good-looking guys. There were five or six empty stools there, so she hopped up onto one. She wiped her hands with a wet wipe from her purse. "Poor thing has mange. You have a lot of cats around here?"

"Yes. They are taking over the island!" He shook his head as he danced between the grill behind him and a large brick oven, pulling out what looked like the most delicious personal margherita pizza that Audrey had ever seen. "Mange, you say?"

She nodded. "Yes, parasitic mites. And there's a good chance other cats have it, too. You probably shouldn't let her in here, just in case. Humans can get it, too, and it's pretty nasty."

He cut and plated the pizza, then set it out for the waitress. "You're a smart one. And how do you know so much?"

"Oh." She tried to suppress the giggle in her throat, but it came out anyway. She blushed. "I'm a veterinarian."

"You are, eh?" He studied her, and then burst out in the loudest laughter Audrey had ever heard. He slapped the glass counter. "You're pulling the leg. You're too young."

For some reason, the dig didn't bother her as much, coming from a guy who was so darn smiley. "No. I promise. And I'm not *that* young."

"Ah. Well. We don't have any vets in town. Our nearest one is over the mountain."

She shrugged. "I guess that's why I'm here. I have to get my license from the board here in Sicily, but once I do, I hope to set up a practice. Maybe even a shelter for rescues."

"Good! That will make you a welcome addition. What's your name?"

"Audrey."

"I'm Giovanni. My friends just call me G, and you're my friend, I hope?" He wiggled his eyebrows animatedly.

"Er …yes. Nice to meet you," she said, surprised that he was still talking to her. Most good-looking guys lost interest after a few minutes, probably because of her tendency to giggle maniacally around them. "Hey, you wouldn't know of any open office buildings, would you? I wanted to set the place up out of my home. But it's kind of in disrepair right now."

He thought for a moment. "I might."

"Thanks, I'd appreciate the help," she said, just happy to have someone to converse with in English, who didn't see this as the biggest mistake ever. She grabbed a menu. "I'm so hungry."

"Then let's get the veterinarian fed. I am the owner of this establishment, and it is an honor to serve you, Dr. Audrey. What can I get you? It is, as you say, on the house."

"Oh, no—"

"I insist!" he said, slapping the counter to end the argument. He waved a spatula at her. "Name it and it is yours, Doctor."

"Well, this is my first meal in Sicily. Can you give me the best thing you make? Something that I will remember for the rest of my life?"

He raised eyebrow. "You're sure?"

She nodded, wondering if it would be a mistake. What if she'd just ordered goat brains?

"All right. You asked for it." His eyes twinkled. "So you're from America, hmm? You buy one of those one-euro houses?"

"Yes, I did," she said. "Piazza Tre."

He hooted. "Yeah? That one's no good." She winced as he grinned and slapped his knee. "Ah, no, they're all good. Just need some love. Are you good with fixing things up?"

"I know my way around a hardware store, yeah," she said, thinking, *Just barely.*

"Well, then, good luck to you. I know what you need," he said, disappearing out of view for a moment, and then returning with a bowl of vegetables swimming in an orange sauce, along with a hunk of crusty bread. He slid it across to her. "This is my own special recipe *ciambotta*. People tell me it makes miracles happen. I think you will like it."

There was steam coming from the shallow bowl, so she spooned just the smallest bit from the side, blew on it, and gently took a sip. Giovanni watched her, waiting for the verdict. The second it hit her tongue, though, she knew she had never tasted anything quite so good in all her life. The vegetables—potatoes, zucchini, tomatoes, and onions—melded so perfectly together in a stew that was a million times better than their individual parts. She quickly drew up another spoonful. "I've never tasted anything like it."

He nodded as if he knew this already. "You know what you should do?"

Have seconds, she thought, as she poured more of the liquid deliciousness down her throat. *Maybe thirds.* "I don't know. What?"

"You don't need an office. When you get your license, you go to them, where they live." He slapped the counter again. He pointed forcefully at her. "You see. You do a good business that way. Be very popular."

She looked up from her bowl. "That's ... actually a good idea." Suddenly, the wheels in her head started to spin. It made total sense. It was a small community, tightly packed together. House calls would be perfect.

"I know it is!" he said. "I am full of good ideas. And here is another one!"

She tried to spoon up more *ciambotta* but she'd reached the bottom of the bowl. She hoped his new idea was more *ciambotta,* but instead, he said, "You're new here. I live here in Mussomeli all my life. I take you out. Show you around. Eh?"

She smiled, hoping that wasn't a date either. Then she threw up her hands. His enthusiasm was contagious. "Sure, why n—"

She stopped when G's eyes lit up over the sight of someone behind her. She turned to see him hurry over and embrace a bald, older man like old friends, after which they spoke to one another in Italian. Audrey only made out a word or two, but she could tell from the tone of their voice and the way the man shook his head and frowned that there was something upsetting him.

Suddenly, G looked at her and his eyes lightened. He presented her to his friend, and she made out her own name and the word "*veterinaria.*" The friend's eyes grew similarly wide, and then he looked at her expectantly, as if there was a question she was supposed to answer.

She looked at him, more curious than ever. "What's going on?"

"Ehm," G started in a low voice. "My friend here. Francisco. His puppy is not well. Acting strange."

"Oh. Strange how?"

"Not eating. Throwing up. Tired. Just sleeps all day."

Audrey looked over at the friend. "*Signore* ... Can I see him? Your dog?"

G smiled and patted her shoulder. "That was what we were hoping you'd say."

CHAPTER THIRTEEN

Francisco's home was only around the corner from G's restaurant. He lived in a small place that Audrey was sure her house could look like, given some time, TLC, and an insane amount of luck. After a stop off at her place to get her medical bag, she met the two men at the home and went inside.

The poor pup, a brindle mutt that looked like he had a bit of shepherd in him, was lying on his side on his bed in the corner of the kitchen, staring at nothing in particular. There was a pot of something delicious-smelling on the stove, but even that didn't seem exciting to him. He didn't even raise his head to look at the strangers.

Francisco murmured something and gesticulated. G translated. "He said if Dante was his normal self, he'd be barking his head off. He's not one for strangers."

"Hmm." Audrey set her bag down and knelt in front of the poor creature. When she offered him her hand, he sniffed without my interest. She petted his side. "It's okay, boy. Let's get you better."

She took out her stethoscope and took his vitals. His heart rate was sluggish, his breathing, labored. From the look of his water and food trays, both full beside the clothes washer, he hadn't the interest. Audrey rummaged in her bag and pulled out a pair of latex gloves, snapping them on. "How long has this been going on?"

G relayed the question to Francisco and translated his answer. "Two days."

Audrey stroked his fur again. Dr. Ferris would probably insist Francisco shuttle over to the next town to find a vet that was licensed. But Dr. Ferris luckily was nowhere on this continent. And though she knew it was risky to be practicing without a license, she wanted to be of help. "It could be something he ate, or a viral infection. I can't make the determination without bloodwork and more tests, which unfortunately, I'm not able to do here," she said, to them both.

G translated, and Francisco shook his head and said something in alarm. "He tells me he doesn't have the means to pay for a vet visit."

Audrey nodded with understanding and pulled the stethoscope from her ears. "If you want my completely honest, off-the-record, unlicensed opinion ... I'd give it a day. He seems well-hydrated, and though he is

67

sluggish, whatever's inside him might just need more time to work its way through. Keep him drinking water, and try to tempt him with bland foods, boiled potatoes, rice, chicken. If he doesn't improve in twenty-four hours, please come and let me know."

"Grazie," Francisco said, after G translated the information to him.

"He will, thank you," G said as he guided her to the door. "You were fantastic. Obviously a very smart lady."

"Oh, well ..." Audrey blushed.

Francisco came up behind her with a giant basket, filled with tomatoes of all colors and shapes. "For you."

Audrey attempted to tell him she didn't need anything, but G ushered her outside before she had a chance to refuse twice. "You never turn down food from a Sicilian. We will always try to feed you. Just don't be stingy with your praise."

Audrey turned back to Francisco on the stoop of his house and waved. "Beautiful! The tomatoes? *Bellisimo!"* She looked at G and whispered, "Was that right?"

He smiled. "You'll be a regular Sicilian yet."

CHAPTER FOURTEEN

On the way back from Francisco's, Audrey took a roundabout route to her home, partly hoping to see more of the village, and partly hoping to avoid dealing with her possessed shower situation as long as possible. She wandered down a similarly narrow street, finding several which were under construction. One, tucked behind a gridwork of scaffolding, was particularly impressive. A man on the second floor was painting the drab gray brick a pretty sea-green.

She stopped to look at it. Obviously, the owners had been here awhile. Maybe in another couple of months, her place would look this good. Unlikely, but there was always hope.

"Take a picture, it'll last longer."

She looked up, shielding her eyes from the glare of the sun, and realized the guy on the scaffolding was looking at her. Her had longish hair and a jaw covered in stubble, bordering on a full beard. Handsome, definitely ... and also holding his paintbrush like a weapon, his brow arched in a superior way.

"What? I'm ..." She stopped, replaying his words in her head. The accent, a slight southern twang. "Wait. You're American?"

He shoved his brush in his tool belt, peeled it off his hips, and climbed down the scaffolding with relative grace. He was slim, wearing cargo shorts, work boots, and a paint-splattered T-shirt. "Nice tomatoes."

"Oh, um ..." Well, that was the type of compliment she expected to get. "Thanks."

He wiped the sweat from his brow, his green eyes boring into hers. "Boston, huh?"

She nodded, her face heating. "How did you know?"

He pointed to the T-shirt she'd changed into. Boston College. Duh. "Only an American would be so forward as to stare at my butt that openly." He eyeballed her bag. "What are you, a doctor?"

She burst out laughing. "I'm a vet. And I was not staring at your butt. I was staring at your house. I was wondering why you chose to paint it that color. It's nice."

"*Riiiight.*" He shrugged. "I like it. That's all. Thought the street could use some brightening up."

"Did you buy it for a dollar? Off a website?"

He grabbed a jug of water and sucked it down greedily. Audrey watched as his Adam's apple bobbed in his thick throat. She tried to avoid staring, but the way he did it was like candy for the eyes. He wasn't just handsome. He was *gorgeous*. No wonder he thought people were staring at his butt. They probably did. Often. "Yeah. Couple weeks ago."

"I did, too!" Although, for someone who'd only moved here a couple weeks ago, his place was in remarkably better condition than hers. "What made you leave ... um, where did you say you were from?"

"I didn't." He didn't seem nearly as pleased to be talking to her as she was to have finally found an American. In fact, he was kind of an egotistical jerk. "I should get back to work."

"Oh. Right. Sorry. Me, too."

He reached for the scaffolding to hoist himself up. Then he looked back and said, "I'm from Charleston. Just had to get away."

She smiled. Well, that was something. "Me, too. Um, I mean, not about Charleston. About getting away." The maniacal giggle came back, but she quickly stifled it. "And you must be handy. Your place looks like it's in much better shape than mine."

He ran an eye over it. "It was a lot worse when I got here. But I wouldn't have bought it if I wasn't a contractor by trade. That'd be stupid."

Audrey's smile faded.

He noticed. For the first time, a smile broke out on his face, baring equally perfect white teeth. "You're kidding, right?"

"I know a lot. My father was a contractor. I just ... it's different, when it's all you." She swallowed. "And I was a little misled. My own fault, really. I thought the place had plumbing, electrical, air conditioning ... a lot more than it actually had. So I think I might be a bit over my head."

"You thought the place had air conditioning?" He gave her a look that said, *You really must be an idiot.*

Her heart sunk. Yes, she probably was an idiot. Somewhere, over the rooftops of the other houses, her phantom shower was calling to her.

"My shower's possessed," she mumbled in a voice so low, she wasn't sure he'd hear her. "And I don't really know much at all about electricity. My dad told me always to hire an expert for that, so he always outsourced it."

He released the scaffolding and looked back at his house. "What are you telling me? You need help?"

She frowned. "No. I wasn't asking you—"

"Yeah, you were. With those little doe eyes of yours?" He smiled, this time genuinely. "It's fine. I never could leave a damsel in distress. I'm too much of a gentleman."

"I'm not in—"

"Fine. You're not." He pulled off his work gloves. "Where do you live? I'll be there in an hour, when I finish the first coat."

"Piazza Tre," she said. "But you really don't—"

He grumbled something and sucked down more water. And actually, his help would be amazing. Maybe then she wouldn't have to spend the evening trying to wrangle up candles so she could see her hand in front of her face tonight.

She extended her hand to him. "Thanks. I appreciate it. I'm Audrey Smart."

He looked at it and laughed. "Smart?" He didn't add anything to that, or else she might have been tempted to knee him in his precious crotch. Instead, he shook her hand, his palms rough with calluses. "Mason."

Letting go, and without warning, he gripped the bottom hem of his shirt and in one fluid movement, lifted it up over his head to reveal too much naked skin than Audrey knew what to do with. She stiffened and tried to look away, but her eyes had a mind of their own. They were glued to him as he easily hoisted himself up the scaffolding and got back to work, his tanned, bare back glistening in the sun.

She physically forced her feet to start moving and pull her up the street. This time, she had to admit, she really was staring.

*

"Not too bad, actually," Mason said an hour later, as he replaced a couple of fuses in the box. "Wiring's pretty good. You might have to have it replaced along the line but it could be worse."

"Really?" Audrey asked hopefully. This was the first good news she'd had about the place all day.

For a few moments, right before she returned to the house, she'd considered telling Maria to stuff those papers. But then she'd returned, dared to look in the bathroom, and realized that the shower phantom had vacated the premises. She flushed the toilet, and it gurgled harmlessly. She tested the shower, and after running for a few minutes,

71

the water seemed almost normal. Still brownish, but definitely a step up from the sludge.

Mason went to the light switch and flipped it. Immediately, warm light filled the kitchen. "And there you go."

Audrey clapped her hands. "Thank you! I can't believe it. I thought I'd be using candles for the next few months."

He shook his head. "No. But if my place was a dollar, this place should've been fifty cents. Where's the rest of it?"

She frowned. "I know. It is small."

"Small? It's a closet. And I'd make sure you take care of that hole," he said, studying the "skylight." "You wouldn't want to fall through that on accident."

She looked up and said, "What hole?" because she thought it sounded cute. Much cuter than, *I actually already fell through that hole.*

He let out a short laugh, just as a commotion rose up outside. They both went out to the front stoop, where a van had parked, unloading a number of men with ladders and tools. It was so close to Audrey's front door, Mason had to squeeze between it and the front stoop. "Looks like you're getting a neighbor," he said.

Audrey watched the men filing in and out of Piazza Due, across the street. "Guess so."

Mason waved at her. "I'll see you. If you need any more help, you know where I am."

He disappeared around the corner as a tiny Fiat pulled up. A woman with stick-straight white-blonde hair and sunglasses popped out. She looked as though she was dressed for a day at the beach, with a tiny tube sundress and a floppy hat in her hand. She slipped a bit on the cobblestone in her kitten heels but righted herself as she dipped her sunglasses to look at the house.

An older worker asked her a question in Italian, and she motioned forcefully and shouted something back at him. Then she rolled her eyes, which landed on Audrey.

Audrey smiled. The woman frowned. She barked something else in Italian at another worker, motioning forcefully with a hand capped with blood-red, clawlike fingernails. She lifted her phone and started to speak into it in perfect American English. "Oh, I'm here. The place is a wreck. Absolute shambles. But I'll make the best of it. You know I always do! No, no, I'm not staying in the house, of course, while it's being renovated, with all those sweaty Sicilians around. I'm booked at a bed-and-breakfast. It's not the Ritz, but it'll have to do ..." She paused, lifted her chin from her phone, and shouted, *"Attento, stupido!"*

She let out a grunt, tottered over to the front of her Fiat, brushed the hood, then growled something under her breath as she ended the call.

Audrey slipped out and waved at her. "You're American? So am I. I'm Audrey. I live here in Tre. We're neighbors."

The woman tilted her head at her and pushed a lock of curly hair behind her ear. She shook Audrey's hand with just the tips of her slim, cold fingers. "I'm Nessa. From L.A. Not here for good. Just here to renovate."

"Oh, so you're not staying once you finish?" Audrey asked, perplexed.

"God, no. You think I'd live in this hellhole permanently?" She rolled her eyes toward the rooftops and fixed her sunglasses back over her eyes. "I have better things to do."

She turned on her heel, flipped her hair, and strutted into the house across the way, doing a quick side-step to get away from a Sicilian worker who'd clearly invaded her bubble.

Audrey looked back at her own place. Her father used to say that homes were a lot like people; they had memories, and hearts, and feelings, too. It was important to nurture them, to only invite the good inside, to love them.

She touched the stone wall. *No. You are not a hellhole. You are mine. And I am going to take care of you. Myself.*

Then she went inside to wait for Maria to come with the papers. Sure, there had been problems, but she'd overcome them. And she'd find a way around the rest of the obstacles, too. She was sure of it. She was ready to sign on the dotted line.

CHAPTER FIFTEEN

"Perfection!" Audrey hammered the final nail into the final wood plank that would seal up her "skylight" between the bedroom and the kitchen, blew on her fingernails, and buffed them on her flannel shirt.

It wasn't perfect, by any means. It was simply a stopgap measure she planned on using until she could get a real carpenter in to create the subfloor, since all the flooring she'd found on the second floor, under the threadbare carpet, was rotted and in need of replacement. Now, instead of worrying about falling into the hole, she'd have to make sure she didn't stub her toe on the protruding wood planks. But at least it would stop anyone downstairs from looking up into her bedroom.

Happy with her work, she slid a roll of old, moldy carpet down the stairs and went down after it to get a glass of water. She scrambled around the roll, shoved herself out onto the first floor, grabbed a pitcher from the mini-fridge, and poured herself a glass. As she was sucking the drink down, she heard it.

The ear-splitting sound of a power saw. It was that, combined with the roar of a drill, a bunch of Italian voices shouting at the top of their lungs, and the beat of some Italian pop music being piped in from someone's radio … that rattled inside her head. So much for the peaceful streets of a Sicilian village.

Audrey peered out a crack in the window. True to her promise, the "neighbor" who was clearly too good for Audrey was nowhere to be seen. But workers were. Dozens and dozens of them. They'd swarmed over the place like ants on a chocolate chip cookie, making as much noise as possible, starting at daybreak.

Her head throbbed. She would've closed the windows but it was too stuffy in the house. Besides, the windows were like Swiss cheese. She finished her glass of water and opened the door, just as some big burly dude screamed something to another crewman who was hanging off the roof, throwing his hammer. The crewman shouted something back and made a rude gesture. Great. *So* gentlemanly.

"Could you please at least try to keep it down?"

The man's eyes drifted to her. He gave her a thorough once-over, then laughed, stuffed a cigar in his mouth, and strutted away. He had absolutely no hair and a gut and biceps the size of Mt. Vesuvius.

Gritting her teeth, she slammed the door. Fine. If they were going to make noise, she would, too.

Only, short of stomping all over the place and grunting really loudly, she didn't know what else to do. If only she had power tools.

She made herself lunch, thinking about that poor little pup she'd seen yesterday. Little Dante. It was a good sign Francisco hadn't paid her a visit. It meant the puppy was probably okay. She'd check in on him, her only patient, later. It was funny, now that she hadn't been practicing in a couple weeks, how much she actually missed it.

Ten minutes later, she was stirred from those thoughts by the same guy, growling something in Italian at the top of his lungs.

She stomped to the door and tore it open. "Would you shut the—"

She stopped when she realized Mason was standing there, knuckles raised, ready to knock.

"Oh, hi," she finished. But apparently, she wasn't finished, because she kept babbling. "Um, hi. Sorry. Hi."

"This a bad time?"

It wasn't for Mason, that was for sure. He looked like he'd just been posing for some *Carpenter's Quarterly* photo shoot, his jeans and tanned arms dotted in paint, sawdust in his hair, his stubble just the right length to make him look rugged without being a mountain man. She gaped, like usual, and of course, giggled maniacally. "No. No. No, it is not."

"Good ..." He eyed her suspiciously, like it was finally dawning on him what made her so repellant to men. "You mentioned you were a vet?"

She blinked. "I did. I mean, I am. Are you ... do you have a pet?"

"No. But I have a situation." He motioned her toward him. "Have a minute?"

He might as well have had her on a string, because she was pulled out of her house so willingly that she nearly forgot to close the door. She went back only because he stopped abruptly, making her nearly slam into his hard chest.

"Bring that ... medical bag thing you have."

Intriguing. She grabbed it, closed up the house, and followed him down the street, back to his place. As they walked, he said, "You making friends already, huh, Boston?"

"The woman across the street from me might as well be renovating the Ritz Carlton," she muttered. "She has like, half the town employed, fixing the place up."

"You sound jealous."

75

"I … totally am," she agreed. Then she shrugged. "Sometimes. But there's a lot to be said by doing things yourself. The hard way. It makes the reward that much sweeter."

He nodded. "That's one way to look at it."

"As long as I don't electrocute myself or unknowingly sell my soul to my demon shower, I think it'll be worth it." They walked another few paces in silence. Truthfully, the second she met him, she'd expected she'd be calling him over to her place about a million times a day. She never expected him to be calling *her*. "What is this about?"

"I found something in my backyard."

She stopped and stared at him, jaw dropped. "You have a backyard? Seriously?" When he shrugged, she said, "*Now* I'm jealous."

Instead of taking her to the door to his little, bright-blue place, he brought her through a small wooden gate to a darling outdoor patio, complete with a little vegetable garden and a very Italian bistro set. Her envy only grew.

But it melted away when she heard the fragile, anguished cries of an animal coming from somewhere near the wrought iron fence. "What's that?"

"That's my problem."

He pushed aside some overgrown vegetation to reveal a tiny red fox, curled into a ball. It was only a juvenile, barely the size of a house cat. It kept letting out little yelps that tore at Audrey's heart. "Oh!"

"That's what I'd thought you'd say. So, can you take it off my hands?"

She gave him a look. "I'm not animal control. This is a wild animal." She peered closer and spied a little bit of blood on his fur. "Oh, the poor thing hurt its leg."

She reached over, careful to avoid the creature's sharp teeth. The animal was surprisingly docile, probably because it was in so much pain. It allowed her to move aside its tail and take a look at the wound.

Studying the surrounding area, she pulled out some antiseptic, gauze, and tape. "Looks like he got it caught on that fence. See how sharp those spikes are, there?"

He touched one of them and when he pulled back, his fingers were coated in red, blood from the poor fox, just as she'd thought. "I was going to change this fence out anyway. Makes this place look like a prison yard."

"At least you have a yard," she muttered, winding the gauze around the fox's tiny leg. She ripped some tape off with her teeth and applied it to the bandage, making it secure. "There we are. Good as new."

She zipped her medical bag, stood up, and brushed her knees.

"I'll send you my bill."

"Wait," he said as she made a move for the door. "Aren't you going to take it with you?"

She froze. "You were serious about that?"

He crossed his arms and leaned against the wall. "Were you serious about the bill?"

She shook her head. It was probably the least she could do, considering all the tasks she'd probably need him for in the coming weeks.

"I *was* serious about the creature. You're a vet. You like furry, wounded things like that. Don't you?" He eyed the animal with more disgust. It'd stopped crying, but now it was just lying there, suspiciously prodding the bandage on its foot. "Besides, I *hate* animals."

"You hate animals," she repeated slowly, trying to force the words into her cranium, but any way she tried, they wouldn't fit. How was that even possible? Especially considering how darn cute this fox was?

He nodded like he hadn't just committed the worst sin against humanity known to man.

Brina had made fun of some of Audrey's Tinder matches, like Bruce, aka the creep from *The Silence of the Lambs.* Yes, there had been a lot of losers. She'd had to deal with men who smelled bad, picked their teeth with a fork at the dinner table, belched loudly, thought wifebeaters were an acceptable first-date outfit, called her *Hot Stuff,* pinched her butt, drove their mother's car to pick her up … and yet as she stood there, gazing at this specimen of human perfection, she realized something.

She had never met a bigger dealbreaker than that.

Audrey moved aside some vines and crouched in front of the poor injured animal. She couldn't let it just stay here, on the property of someone who clearly had no soul. She shrugged off the flannel shirt she'd been using as a jacket and laid it down, then gently lifted the fox into it, cradling him there, in a little nest.

"Fine, I'll take him," she said, scooping him into her arms. "*If* you agree to help me with my subflooring."

He raised an eyebrow, ready to argue, but then looked back at the fox and his jaw tightened in disgust. "Fine. Good deal." Mason held the door open for her as she stepped out of his garden. "Thanks for your help, Dr. Doolittle."

She gave Mason a wave with her middle finger a little higher than the others, and didn't look back. Her attention was on the fox, who was now curled up warmly, snuggling against her breast. It opened its jaw and yawned, and was that a smile on its face? So stinkin' cute.

Total dealbreaker.

But at least she'd get a new subfloor out of it.

*

"All right. One … two … three … *heave!"*

She used all her strength to yank the old, musty roll of carpeting out of the stairwell. With one final yank, it finally slid out into the pseudo-foyer in a big cloud of dust.

Audrey choked and reached for her glass of water. As she did, she nearly tripped over the fox, who'd scampered from its nest in the kitchen to see what she was up to. She had to do a little skip-dance to avoid injuring it worse.

"What does the fox say?" she grumbled at him as she slumped into the only chair in the place, a seventies-style avocado-green plastic thing near the kitchen table. "Well, whatever it does say, I wish you'd say it louder, because I almost flattened you back there. You're sly, Nick Wilde."

He looked up at her, tilting his head as if he was trying to understand.

"Forget it. You look better, at least," she said, pouring some more water into the dish she'd gotten for him. She didn't have anything but soda crackers that she'd swiped from G's restaurant, so she gave a couple of those to him, too. "Or were you playing the dude in distress so some hot girl would come to your rescue?"

He sniffed at the crackers and slowly stuck his tongue out to taste them.

Her eyes wandered back to that moldy excuse for a rug. Now, all she had to do was drag it out the door and down the street about a quarter mile, to the dumpster at the end of the road. Her already aching muscles protested at the mere thought. Maybe she could get Luca to come by with his hardware cart and help.

No. She'd come here to do this herself, not rely on a bunch of men to do her dirty work. Besides, there were other things she'd probably need their expertise for, later. Even … gasp. Even the animal-hater.

"Don't give me that look," she said to the fox, who seemed to be saying to her, *Why waste time with him when you've got all this cuteness?* "True. But he's the reason we've got light in this house. I have to admit, he did a pretty bang-up job."

Trying to psych herself up for the haul, she stood up and pulled open the door, only to find a pile of construction waste on her front stoop. She certainly had enough of that on her own ... but she was sure this stuff didn't belong to her site, especially since one of the pieces of waste was a toilet that looked even nicer than the new one she'd just had installed. As she poked her head out to investigate, more of it came flying down in a puff of brown dust, nearly hitting her right between the eyes.

She backed away and spied Biceps through the haze. "Hey! What are you doing?"

He had another cigar crammed between his lips and was sucking on it, ignoring her as he spouted more directives in Italian to workers above. The junk—rotten bits of wood, old plaster, nails, and an assortment of other garbage, kept raining down, right on her stoop. A particularly large hunk of old piping fell like a boulder, inches from her feet. The fox had been peering out from behind her legs, but it yelped when the thing landed, shaking the foundation of the building.

The man—who must've been the foreman of the job, considering how much supervising he was doing, and little else—turned toward her, but seemed more interested in the fox than in her.

She waved a hand at him. "Hello? Watch it! You can hurt someone with this stuff! And I hope you're not just going to leave this here?"

He came up close to her, too close, and pulled the cigar from his mouth with a resounding pop. "That your wild animal?"

Surprised both that he spoke English and by the question, she was momentarily knocked off her game. She looked down. "No. I'm a vet. I just found him. He's—"

"Not supposed to be in your house, *si*?"

"What?" She looked up, at the shapes of the workers, who were finally silent, watching their interaction. Down the street, people had begun to poke their heads out of their doors, as if they were getting ready for the daily entertainment. "Well, it's—"

"You keep harassing my crew and I'll report you to the city. It's illegal to keep wild animals around here."

Audrey stared at him, dumbfounded. So he was going to go there, was he? "*Me? Harassing them?*" Her jaw dropped in indignation. "You're the one throwing your junk all over my property and not cleaning it up. You make noise all hours of the day and you don't seem to have respect for anyone else!"

More shutters were being thrown open, and a couple stopped on the street to watch.

The foreman sucked on his cigar, leaned in close, and blew a smelly cloud of smoke into her face. "You're not paying me, *signorina*. So I don't have to listen to anything you tell me."

She stood there, face heating, hands shaking, stomach twisting. She willed the volcano inside her not to blow its top off, but even so, it brewed in her, dangerously close to the point of no return. It took all her strength to step back, grab the door, and slam it in his face.

The fox looked at her with a question in his eyes, but she simply trudged back up the stairs. Maybe she'd call it a day and turn in early, if the jerks across the street wouldn't keep her up all night.

She'd worry about disposing of the damn moldy carpeting tomorrow. Right now, all she wanted to do was dream up revenge schemes. She'd have to do *something*. She couldn't just let things drag on like this.

CHAPTER SIXTEEN

Audrey didn't get to sleep.

Just as expected, the construction crew across the way continued their racket even into the midnight hour. Audrey sat on her lumpy mattress, yawning and stewing, stewing and yawning. Sure, they'd done this every night since they arrived, but now, Audrey couldn't stop thinking that they were doing it *because* of her little outburst. Just to spite her.

And she'd had every right to put her foot down! Was it such a crime to want a little peace and quiet? They were absolutely in the wrong. Absolutely.

As she lay there in the darkened apartment, listening to the power saw cutting its way into her head, plans for sabotaging their renovations filtered through her head. She realized she was grinding her teeth to little nubs and relaxed her jaw. She picked up her phone and called Brina.

Her sister greeted her with, "Wait. Why are you calling me at a normal hour? This is so unlike you."

Audrey yawned. "What time is it there?"

"Seven in the evening. I just put Byron down to bed. So that means it's … wait. Why are you up at one in the morning?"

"Because of this." She held up her phone to the air to give her sister a listen. "Did you hear that?"

"Of course I did. What is that? Are you being attacked by bees?"

"No. The renovation across the street is, apparently, a twenty-four-seven thing. All they do is work. I haven't slept in days."

"Oh, god. That's horrible, sweetie. I'm sorry."

"Their house wiring is attached to mine. I can reach out my bedroom window and snip it. I'm seriously considering this. So I'm calling to ask you to talk me down from the ledge."

"No. No no no," Brina said immediately. "Knowing you, you'd fall out your window or electrocute yourself, and then get thrown in an Italian prison. I hear they don't feed foreigners in places like that."

She winced. But as always, Brina dropped the truth bomb.

"Seriously. Get some noise cancelling headphones and call it a day. Otherwise, how are things going there?"

"They're okay. I have a toilet. And electricity now."

There was a pause. "Um, Audrey? You sound like you're living in a third world country. Those are not things to be happy about. Those are things most of the earth's population happily takes for granted."

"Well, it's progress. You know what Dad said. Rome wasn't built in a day. I'm getting there. And other than the jerky neighbors, it's really kind of nice. Most of the people are nice. Can you believe that slimeball actually said he'd turn me in for harboring a wild animal?"

"Uh-oh. What poor-and-abandoned did you decided to adopt now?"

Audrey pressed her lips together. Yes, she had a bit of an affinity for taking in strays, ever since the inchworm she named "Lovey" in first grade. She'd cleared out her Barbie Dreamhouse to give him a place to live. So what? "A fox. I call him Nick."

"Oh, god, you named him already?"

"Yes. After the fox in *Zootopia,* only the greatest movie about—"

"Aud. I have kids. I know Disney's entire catalogue these days better than I know Sephora's newest colors. Unfortunately. The problem is that you named the creature. That's like saying it belongs to you."

"I couldn't just throw him out. He was injured."

"Bah. You don't need that extra responsibility when you have a house to get in order. I know what would *really* make things better for you. A man. Any cute Sicilian guys sweep you off your feet?"

She thought of G. "Well ... there's one. He's a chef. And then there's a neighbor, but he's from America. And he hates animals. Plus he's ridiculously full of himself."

"How very American. Tell me more about the chef. That sounds promising."

"I don't know. He mentioned taking me out to see the sights, but that's about it."

"Guess you don't have a lot of time for that, huh?"

Audrey sighed. "Right. There are a lot of young foreigners coming here, fixing things up. So far, I think I met more ex-pats than actual Sicilians. It's not exactly what I pictured ... in a way, it's like frat row. I guess I couldn't escape America, even if I tried."

"I am sure it'll get better when you fix the place up some more and you find your way around town. Maybe with the help of that hot Sicilian chef?"

"Who knows? I'm not holding my breath. In fact, the last thing I'm thinking about is making a love connection." She sunk down against the pillows and gazed out the open shutters, to the moonlit sky. "I'm just being miserable because I'm so tired."

"Then get some sleep."

She realized that the power saw had ceased operations, and finally, the night was quiet, with nothing but the sound of crickets chirping and the wind, whistling through the empty streets. That was nice. Yes, if it weren't for her neighbors, there'd be a lot to love about this. She just needed to concentrate on that. "All right. Good night."

Ending the call, Audrey went to set her phone on the floor beside her when she saw a shape moving in the darkness. Before she could let out the scream that had lodged itself in her throat, a large furry mass jumped onto her stomach. She let out a half-"oof!", half-wail, and nearly flung the thing out the window, until she realized what it was.

"Oh. Nick," she whispered, settling back down. The fox, as if he'd been her pet for ages, curled on the pillow beside her. She reached over and stroked his fur. "What do you say we get some sleep?"

He didn't answer, and she didn't wait. She fell asleep almost instantly.

*

Audrey was in a massive home overlooking the white-capped bay, on a gray, dreary day in January. It was snowing, and there was no heat yet in the house, but her father had brought in a space heater, and so she kept returning there to keep her fingers warmed.

"All right, kid. Just a little more sanding and this wall will be smooth as a baby's bottom."

She giggled. Her father may have called her "kid," but he didn't treat her like one. He'd given her her own toolbelt and tools, not prissy pink "girl" ones—real, contractor-grade instruments, like his own. And whenever she got back from school and his crew members had to go home to their families, he'd stay later, inspecting their work and teaching Audrey lessons she hadn't learned in the classroom.

Brina moaned from beside the space heater as she finished her algebra. "It's almost dark. Isn't it time to go home yet?"

Miles Smart laughed. "In a bit, Bri." He turned on a lamp and motioned Audrey to the side of the bench. "Let's move the workbench over there. Ready?"

She nodded eagerly, and the two of them picked it up. She may have held one side, sort of, but he did all the heavy lifting.

He handed her the sandpaper. "All right. You do that side. Just like I showed you."

She took the sandpaper and moved it back and forth over the plaster. "Like this?"

"Yep. Good job. Keep it going. Put some muscle into it."

She smiled at him, and he gazed back at her, such love and admiration in his eyes.

But suddenly, his eyes widened. He seemed to concentrate on something behind her, his face twisting into something like horror and surprise. His mouth opened to the shape of an O and called out her name, but it sounded as though he was underwater, miles away. She reached for him, but he backed away, then, in a blink, shattered into a million little pieces before her eyes.

Audrey sat up in bed, her heart pounding.

Her sudden motion made the fox look up, but he quickly rolled over and went back to sleep. She stared out at the lightening sky, with only a few remaining pinpoint stars, thinking of her father. She'd thought of him a lot in the years since he left without any explanation, but eventually, she'd tucked those painful memories away. They only served to remind her that she'd been abandoned. Now, with the renovation, it seemed like they were all coming to the forefront.

Now, more than ever, she wanted to know where he went, and why.

CHAPTER SEVENTEEN

The following morning, Audrey was up before the sun. Her phantom shower must have been exorcised, because it behaved long enough to give her a thorough washing, and by six o'clock, she was dressed and brewing strong coffee. She took a mug of it outside to inspect the damage from her neighbor's renovation and was pleasantly surprised that they'd cleaned everything up. And the foreman was obviously a hard worker—his truck was already parked at the corner.

Audrey sipped her coffee and let the bitter heat sting her tongue. She'd been rash. Maybe he was a good guy, after all. It might have been a misunderstanding. A culture gap.

She'd already been planning to try to smooth things over with him, even before she'd gone to sleep last night. She could never let things like this lie and fester. She'd gone to the market yesterday and bought a cask of expensive, artisan olive oil, which had run her twenty-five euros. She'd give it to him. A peace offering.

Holding the tiny, wicker-wrapped glass jar, she took a step for the stoop and tangled herself in Nick's long, furry tail.

"Whoa, whoa, whoa." She wagged a finger at him. "Get back in there. You're what got me into trouble in the first place."

The fox turned obediently and went inside, and she felt guilty for scolding him. It wasn't his fault, either. After what the foreman had said, though, she was extra nervous about letting anyone see him in her house.

As she closed the door behind her, the door across opened. It was the blonde American, Nessa, dressed in butt-hugging running shorts and a bra top, hair in a long, sleek ponytail.

Audrey waved. "Hi, Nessa. Nice morning!"

She glanced Audrey's way as she tried to fix some earbuds into her ears and sighed. "I guess."

"So, are you living in the house now?"

"For now. Ernesto and his crew finished most of it last night."

Ernesto. So that was big and beefy's name. "Speaking of Ernesto … I saw his truck. Is he around? I wanted to discuss something with him."

85

She frowned. "I'm sure you do. Don't think you're going to steal him from me. The last thing I want is every other house on this block looking like mine. That'll send the resale rates plummeting."

"No, I wasn't. I just—"

She sliced her hand through the air. "I have no idea. I don't pay attention to their comings and goings, as long as they get my work done. He isn't in my house. If he's anywhere, he's probably in the yard. I told him I needed that cleared out."

So she had a backyard, too. Life wasn't fair. "Did they do a nice job inside?"

"Passable. Someone will probably want this disaster. As for me, the shorter I stay here, the better. Once I finish giving it my magic touch, I'm out."

"Oh. Are you an interior designer?"

She patted her chest, clearly offended. "You don't know who I am? I'm Nessa Goodroe."

She said the name like it should've rung a bell. Audrey just stared blankly.

"Hello? One of the best. I have close to two million Instagram followers. I'm in talks with HGTV to have my own show."

"Ohhh. Okay. Sorry. I don't pay much attention to—"

"Got to go!" She jogged off down the street, her ponytail swishing behind her.

Still holding her peace offering at chest level, she went across the street to the little gate between the houses. It creaked open, providing an impossibly narrow passage between the two crumbling walls. She squeezed through it, and out into a little courtyard on the cliffside. Audrey gaped, and again she had the feeling she'd gotten the short end of the stick when it came to picking properties. Yes, her own view from her second floor was scenic, but the view from the overgrown patio was spectacular.

Spectacular, if a little … dangerous. She only took a few steps before she started to get vertigo, because past a low stone wall was a steep, precipitous drop that made her insides wobble.

She studied the red brick patio. No work had been done out here, that was for sure. The weeds had grown into a hopeless tangle that a machete wouldn't cut through. And no Ernesto.

Audrey was about to spin and head back the way she came when she noticed something stuck among the brown brambles bordering the stone wall.

A boot. A man's large, heavy work boot.

A queasy feeling planted itself in Audrey's stomach. Forgetting the olive oil in her hands, she rushed to the stone wall. She picked up the boot and peered down over the edge of the cliffside, fighting her wooziness.

There, on a stone outcropping about forty feet below, was the sprawled body of Biceps himself, a halo of black blood around his head.

CHAPTER EIGHTEEN

At first, she thought she was seeing things. Maybe those sleepless nights were catching up with her. She blinked and looked closer. The image didn't change.

"Oh God," she said aloud, stifling a scream. Her skin prickled with heat, despite the chill in the air. The vertigo threatened to take over. "Oh God oh God oh God."

Still holding the boot and staring at the grisly sight in front of her, sure it would be tattooed on her brain for the rest of her life, she reached into the pocket of her jeans and pulled out her cell phone. Instinctively, she dialed 911, then listened dumbly for about thirty seconds to the sound of nothingness.

You're not in America, remember? some still-sane part of her brain reminded her. Right. Maria had given her a bunch of pamphlets with helpful information, and she'd paged through them, but she'd never actually believed she'd be calling emergency. There was a one in the number. Maybe two of them. And a ... three?

Frantically, she tried all different combinations of the numbers, each failed attempt eliciting a cry of frustration. She was just about to give up when she poked in 113 and someone answered with, *"Qual è la sua emergenza?"*

Emergency. She gripped the phone tighter. "English? Please tell me you speak English? There's a dead guy here. At least I think he's dead. He fell from the side of the cliff."

There was a pause. Then the operator said, *"Cosa è successo?"*

Audrey let out a cry of frustration. "I can't understand you!"

She peered over the side of the cliff for barely a blink, hoping that the sight would prove to be only a figment of her imagination. Wrong. The more she looked, the more nauseated she became. The bitter taste of the coffee bubbled in the back of her throat, threatening to make a reappearance. Meanwhile, the woman on the other end of the phone continued to speak Italian, so fast, Audrey's head spun.

"I don't understand," she moaned, backing away. "Piazza Due. Ambulance-o. *Por favor. Gracias.*"

Suddenly, a shadow descended over her and the phone was scooped out of her hand. Audrey whirled in alarm, sure she was about to be pushed, and saw Nessa there, barely winded and basking in a healthy runner's glow. She hopped onto the top of the stone wall and glanced over, fearless, then spoke Italian into the phone. Then she ended the call gave Audrey a superior smile. "Sicily," she said, pointing. "Spain's a little ways that way."

She tossed the phone back to Audrey. Still shaking and holding Ernesto's boot, Audrey fumbled to catch it and realized she'd dropped the cask of olive oil on the ground. It'd shattered, spilling oil and shards of glass all over the reddish stone.

Nessa looked down at the boot in Audrey's trembling hand, then met her eyes. "Soooo, friend … what have *you* been up to?"

*

The *Polizia* arrived shortly afterward, lights flashing and sirens wailing. Until that moment, Audrey hadn't even known that Mussomeli had much of a police force. Several uniformed men swarmed the area, speaking urgently in Italian.

Numb, her head now pounding with a migraine, Audrey tried to skirt away from the chaos that had descended upon the small house on the cliffside, but a large officer blocked the narrow passage. He started shouting directives to her, making her head throb more. "What? I'm sorry. I don't speak Italian."

He said, "Another American, eh?" and rolled his eyes. "You discovered the body, yes?"

She nodded.

"Then you need to stay right here. The detective in charge, Eduardo DiNardo, will want to question you."

"Uh. Okay."

She shrunk backward, trying to get out of the way of the many officers, but everywhere she tried to plant herself, she found more of them. She pinballed around until she finally located a spot among the weeds, in a safe place away from the cliff where she wouldn't meet the same fate as Ernesto.

Meanwhile, Nessa stood in the center of the patio, like a sun with all the policemen her orbiting planets. She spoke in a fluid Italian to her audience, looking more like a celebrity giving a guest lecture than a witness being questioned about an accident. As she spoke, she kept gesticulating toward Audrey and saying, *assassina.*

Audrey didn't take more than a few seconds to make the translation on her own. It wasn't hard, considering the way the police had begun looking at her like gum on the bottom of someone's shoe. *Either she's calling me an ass, which ... fine, I'd actually prefer, right now ... or ... she's telling them that I'm... I'm a ...*

Audrey straightened and approached the fray. "Wait, wait, wait ... what is she saying?"

One of the men broke through to her. Unlike the others, he was wearing a suit and tie and looked more like an investment banker than a police officer, except for the unmistakable bulge of a gun under his blazer. "What is your name, please?"

"Audrey. Audrey Smart. I live across the street." She hugged herself tightly. "I'm not in trouble, am I?"

"I'm Detective DiNardo. Can I ask you some questions?" he said, in fairly good English.

She nodded. "Yes, but I don't understand. Isn't this some horrible accident?"

"It's possible, *signorina.*"

"Doctor, actually."

He eyed her doubtfully. "Doctor. But the fact is that the boot is suspicious, and there are scuffs in the dirt near the wall that suggest a possible struggle. We'll know more, of course, when we get a look at the body." He tilted his head and paged through a little notebook. "You discovered the body, is that right?"

She nodded, wringing her hands together. "Um, yes. It's ... you see ... my first dead body." She started to hyperventilate.

The detective ignored her distress. "And Signorina Goodroe said that she found you, holding the boot?"

"Well, yes. I picked it up when I saw it, but ..." Her blood went cold. She shook her head. "I didn't push him, if that's what you're ... uh, oh God. Whatever she's saying and you're thinking is wrong. I'm not a ... I have no reason to ..." She waved a hand in front of her face, trying to suck air into her lungs, but it felt like they were closing up on her.

Still oblivious to her impending fainting spell, he gave Audrey a doubtful look. "You live across the street. And what inspired you to come over here so early?"

"Well, I um, was looking for the foreman. Ernesto. I just wanted to talk to him."

He scribbled something down in his pad. "About?"

"We'd gotten into an argument last night, and ..." Audrey trailed off and bit her tongue. The last thing she needed was to give him more reason to suspect her.

Too late to backpedal. "Argument, hmm? About what?"

"Nothing, really. They were noisy and messy, and they'd left trash on my front stoop. I wanted to smooth things over with him. That was all. I swear."

"Smooth things over?" he repeated.

Maybe he hadn't been eyeing her with doubt, maybe it was normal for police officers to be suspicious of everything everyone told them, but Audrey couldn't get it out of her head that he wanted to see her rot away in an Italian prison for the rest of her life.

God, this was so surreal, she was having trouble believing this wasn't the continuation of that vivid dream she'd had earlier, of her dad.

"Yes! And not by pushing him off the side of a cliff. Who would do that? I actually wanted to thank him for cleaning it up." He didn't say anything in response, since he was too busy scribbling on his notepad, so she felt the need to fill the silence. "I mean, really. I, um, called the police, didn't I? I stayed here until you guys came. If I'd pushed him, wouldn't I get away from here, as quick as I could?"

"You may have been trying to," Nessa's voice called from across the patio. Audrey and every other person turned to look at Nessa, who was lounging on the edge of the stone wall, like she was trying to get a suntan. Apparently, when she spoke, everyone listened. "She was backing toward the exit. Maybe it was only because I got there that she couldn't run. I came back for my sunglasses, that's why. I caught her red-handed. Still holding the boot."

Audrey's jaw dropped. "What? No, that's—"

"The truth is that the body hasn't been there that long," DiNardo explained. "We'll know more, obviously, when we get the coroner's report. Did you happen to see anyone else while you were outside? Anyone behaving suspiciously?"

Audrey wished she had. But she'd seen absolutely no one. For a moment, she wondered if she could lie, create some phantom figure in black, just to take the heat off herself, but then she decided she was already in enough trouble as it was. "No. No one."

"Me neither!" Nessa called. "Not a soul."

Audrey glared at her.

"I'll need your passport," DiNardo said.

"It's back at my house," she explained lamely, every hair on her body standing at attention. When he moved aside to let her through, indicating that he'd go with her, like she was some prisoner that he couldn't let out of his sight, she repeated, "I'm not in trouble, am I?"

She was hoping for *of course not, you're clearly innocent!* But he simply said, "Just following procedures, *signorina.*"

All the officers watched her as she made her way down the narrow passage and across to her house, DiNardo on her heels. *Oh, God, I am in trouble. Italian prison, here I come.*

She paused with her hand on the door of her home, when a thought suddenly occurred to her. Nick. *They're going to arrest me for harboring a wild animal, and keep me in prison while they build their murder case against me. I am so screwed.*

But suddenly, Nessa burst out of the gate, shouting and waving her arms wildly. "I don't care! You're serious about this? Really? Shutting down my renovations? That's BS!"

DiNardo turned to defuse the situation, hands up. "Just until we can conclude our investigations. This is a crime scene."

"Well, how long will that take?" Nessa snapped.

Making no sudden moves, Audrey quickly pushed open the door. Sure enough, Nick stuck its muzzle out. She nudged him back gently, grabbed her purse from the hook near the front door, and appeared back on the stoop in a matter of seconds, even before DiNardo could notice she'd been gone.

She rummaged through her purse and pulled out the little blue booklet with the single Italian stamp inside. "Here it is!"

DiNardo took it from her. "It goes without saying that until our investigation is complete, you're not to go anywhere."

She nodded. "I understand. No leaving the country."

"No. No leaving Mussomeli."

"Oh. Okay." She found it hard to breathe, as if the walls of this town were caving in on her. Across the street, Nessa scowled at her and mouthed, *Great job, assassina.*

Never had Audrey wanted to flip someone off more. Upset about a delay in renovations? Nice first world problem to have. But this was Audrey's *life* hanging in the balance. Her career. Her family. Her entire freaking *life*.

Now, even if Audrey desperately wanted to go home … she couldn't. She couldn't even go on a drive outside the city. She was a prisoner.

But as she fielded suspicious glances from all sides, she knew that was far from the worst thing she could be.

CHAPTER NINETEEN

"I'm sorry, who is this?" Audrey asked, clutching the phone to her ear as she scampered around the house, peering out whatever window she could for shreds of evidence to how the investigation was proceeding.

A very accented voice said, "I have a goat who is sick. My friend Francisco, he say you help?"

Oh. A house call. Yes. This was probably just what she needed to get her mind off the investigation. Even if she didn't technically have her license, she could still help a sick goat. "Yes. I can. What seems to be the problem?"

"Goat, he no eat. He very old."

"All right. Well, I can come right away," she said. It was better than slowly being driven insane, doing circles around her house. "What street are you on?"

"No street. I'm in Polizzelo. You come?"

"Sure. If I can find the …" She trailed off as it dawned on her. "Wait. Where is that … is that another … another town?"

"Si. Not far from Mussomeli. You come?"

She frowned, remembering DiNardo's words. "Actually. I don't think I can. I … don't have any way of getting there." At least, it sounded better than *I'm the main suspect in a murder investigation.* "I'm sorry."

She ended the call and sighed. It was probably better that she stayed on the straight and narrow, anyway. She didn't want to give the police any more reasons to suspect her.

Her eyes went to Nick. She'd probably have to get rid of him, too.

If only he wasn't so dang cute. She'd sooner saw her own arm off than just let him go. With that little limp of his, he'd probably be devoured by a hawk the second she let him out.

So she spent most of the afternoon slowly going insane, spying on the police investigation.

Maybe it was that feeling of claustrophobia, but Audrey couldn't stay in her house a second longer. The minute the last police car pulled away, she rocketed out of her front door and practically ran to La Mela

Verde. She told herself she wanted a cup of G's *ciambotta,* but really, she just wanted to be able to breathe normally again.

But the face behind the counter didn't belong to G. It was a young woman with hoop earrings and a pink stripe in her hair. Maybe it was Audrey's imagination, but when the woman looked at her, she could've sworn she saw the same suspicion that the police officers had given her.

Turning out of the place, she wandered randomly to the only other person she could think of.

Unfortunately, that was *Are you looking at my butt, I hate animals* Mason.

He smirked as if she was paying him a booty call when she arrived like a lost lamb on his front stoop. "Couldn't keep away, could you, Boston?"

She scowled at him.

He checked behind her. "Where's your oh-so-cute sidekick? Don't tell me you got rid of him?"

"I have bigger things to worry about."

He raised an eyebrow. "What? Your father told you that you had to outsource the plumbing, too?"

"Just let me in," she muttered, pushing past him and into his house.

He turned on her. "No sexual favors required. Just tell me what you need. A new sink?"

"Don't even go there." She shot him a grossed-out look and scanned the place. It lacked a woman's touch, but everything was new. The rooms were bigger. Nicer. Better situated. To top it all off, he had a darn garden. Something so shallow shouldn't have bothered her, considering *La Polizia* wanted her head on a platter, but somehow, it only made her feel worse. "Do you have something to drink?"

"Yep." He went to the tiny fridge under the counter. "Water? San Pellegrino? Orange jui—"

"You have anything stronger?"

He closed the fridge, pushed aside a curtain to reveal a stocked pantry, and pulled out a cask of red wine, possibly something he might have pressed himself. She didn't care. She needed something to take the edge off. He poured a little—too little, in Audrey's eyes—into two stemless wine glasses and handed one to her.

She sucked it down before he finished saying, "*Salud.*"

The empty glass quivered in her hand. He eyed her with much of the same suspicion the police officers had. He didn't offer her more. Instead, he pointed her to a small chair in his kitchen. She slumped into it.

"So ... what's the deal, Boston? You been spending too much time talking to that possessed shower of yours?"

She shook her head miserably. "The thing is, I think I'm suspect *numero uno* in a murder investigation."

His eyes flooded with interest, but it wasn't the kind she was hoping for. She wanted compassion. She wanted concern. She wanted Perry Mason to swoop down and tell her everything would be all right. But *this* Mason, the Mason she was stuck with, simply leaned forward like a highway rubbernecker at a grisly pile-up. "You don't say. Who'd you off?"

Her scowl deepened.

He held out two hands in surrender. "Sorry. Just kidding." He drained his own glass and smirked, showing two adorable dimples, which made it impossible to hate him. "But sincerely, now, girl ... who died, and why would they think a little thing like you is responsible?"

She wasn't sure that was a compliment. Knowing the little she did of him, she didn't think so. Was it possible for him to compliment anything other than his reflection? "The foreman who was working on the house across the street. He fell off the cliff at the back of the house, and he died."

"Yeah? Was there a lot of blood?"

She ignored the question, because yes, there was a lot of blood, but if she thought about it too much she was bound to get queasy again. "I was arguing with him the night before, because he was making all this noise and leaving a bunch of crap in front of my house, so I'd had it. I tore into him, and everyone on the street saw. So I have motive. And then I went out back to have a talk with him, and I found the body. Supposedly he'd only died a few minutes before I got there. So I don't have an alibi. Motive plus no alibi? Boom. Instant suspect." She slumped in the chair, feeling worse.

"Really? Wild." He shook his head, poured himself another glass of wine. It was only when he caught her pouting at his full glass like a stray puppy outside a meat shop that he poured her one. "What makes them think it wasn't an accident?"

"I don't know. There were signs of a struggle, I guess." She left out the part about her being caught with the dead man's boot in her hand.

"Yeah? That's too much."

She waited for him to give her some words of encouragement, or at least list all the reasons why there was no way she could've committed the crime. But he just scratched his jaw and motioned to his overflowing trash can.

"You happen to figure out when the trash pick-up is around here? Sometimes the guys come on Tuesday. Sometimes on Wednesday. I can't keep it straight."

She stared at him, hoping he wasn't serious. But he stared back at her, expectant, waiting for the answer.

Really? Her life was in the balance. Did she give two flying figs about trash pick-up?

She stood up. "You know what. I think I'll just go …"

Her stomach roiled. Like she wanted to go back to the scene of the crime. Well, close enough. He didn't stop her. He simply said, "See you, Boston. Or if I don't, guess I'll assume you're in the pen."

Audrey sighed. "Thanks for the pep talk. I appreciate it."

"Hey," he said as she headed out the door, hands in the pockets of her jacket, head down. Back to her home, back to reality, back to the place where a man had just lost his life.

She looked up.

He motioned her forward. "Give me your phone."

She handed it to him without question. He took it and started to work his thumbs over the display. Only after a few seconds of this did she think to question what he was doing. "What are you …"

"Giving you my number."

"So you can be my one phone call?"

He handed it back to her. "No. Just in case you need me. For anything."

Well … that was kind of sweet.

"You didn't do it, right? So what do you have to worry about? You're going to be fine."

She nodded and let out the breath she'd been holding. If only she could feel that confident.

On the way home, though, again, it felt like everyone was staring at her. Before, she felt like an outsider. Now, she felt like a criminal.

And if she didn't want to spend her life in that Italian prison, she couldn't just sit around, waiting for them to clear her name. She needed to do something to clear it herself.

CHAPTER TWENTY

Audrey tried to ignore the yellow crime scene tape across the street as she walked up the street to her house. There was one police car parked outside, but there was nobody else on the street to give her the stink-eye or call her an *assassina*.

She couldn't help feeling like she was being followed.

After a few steps, she stopped and stood, frozen, when she heard the unmistakable sound of feet, sweeping on the stone street.

Whirling, she looked. Nothing.

She sighed. This was all the work of her friendly neighbor. Now, she was paranoid.

Really, Nessa was a piece of work. If there had ever been any hope of them becoming the kind of neighbors who shared gossip at their front stoops and passed casseroles to one another, that was gone now. The sooner Nessa could flip her house to real neighbors, *caring* neighbors who didn't accuse her of crimes she didn't commit, the better.

The sound came again. Someone was *definitely* following her. Her arms prickled with goosebumps.

She took a deep breath and whirled fast, catching a spot of red in her peripheral vision as it zoomed behind a potted plant on someone's stoop.

Nick.

"Come on out," she said, crossing her arms. As if understanding her perfectly, it poked its head around the pot and then carefully made its way to her. She let out a tsk. "Didn't I lock you up in the house? How did you get out?"

In reply, he slipped between her legs, wrapping his bush tail around her calf, like a cat wanting to be petted. Audrey looked up and down the street. The last thing she needed was the police seeing her harboring a wild animal. Then she scooped it into her arms and took it quickly to her front door.

A sick feeling settled over Audrey as she entered her little home, set Nick free to roam around her kitchen, and looked around. Sure, it wasn't much. But it had to be better than prison.

She wasn't in the mood to tackle the next thing on her renovation list. Instead, her mind kept wandering to Ernesto. Who could've done that? Did he have any enemies? Likely. It wasn't nice to speak ill of the dead but the guy had been a jerk to her. He probably had *loads* of enemies. Maybe he'd been involved in shady dealings with someone. Maybe he'd gotten on someone's bad side.

Her thoughts spiraled out to a few days ago, when she'd caught one of the crewmen yelling at him and flipping him off.

Of course!

She grabbed her kettle and put it on the burner. When it whistled, she poured herself a cup of tea, fetched her notepad out of her purse, and sat down, thinking.

Just because she and Nessa hadn't seen anyone else there didn't mean anything. The killer could've gone into the backyard and pushed Ernesto in mere seconds. Whoever had killed Ernesto was likely expecting him to be there alone. He probably didn't know that Nessa had moved in. Or maybe he knew she took a morning run and wouldn't be there.

And a murder like that could've been unplanned. He and whoever the killer was could've argued and struggled, or maybe it was an accident. He fell, and the person who did it got scared and ran off.

But if they had argued, wouldn't Audrey or Nessa have heard something? Wouldn't she have heard him shout? Audrey had been listening, too, because she'd been surprised not to hear much noise coming from over there. Her house was like Swiss cheese, so even the smallest sounds seemed to travel to her windows.

So Audrey was convinced that whatever had happened, it hadn't been a regular row, like the one she'd had with him earlier, where they'd accumulated an audience. Maybe everything happened so fast, and the real killer was at home, now, feeling guiltier and guiltier by the second. Maybe it was only a matter of time before he turned himself in.

That didn't help Audrey feel any better. She finished her tea and scribbled some more notes.

She scribbled the word *CREWMEN* down on the pad and circled it thickly. Yes, she'd have to talk to them, one by one, narrowing them down. Just like a regular Sherlock.

Just then, there was a knock on her door.

She nudged Nick into the bathroom and cracked the door to find a tall police officer standing there, with a mop of dark hair that made the rest of his skinny body look like the handle. He had to have been fresh out of his teens, with the acne on his cheeks to prove it. "Signorina Smart?"

She opened the door a little wider, but not too wide. "Yes?"

He started to speak in Italian, and she held up her hands.

"Hold on. I'm sorry. I'm Italian 101. I don't understand."

He smiled big, bearing perfectly straight white teeth, a contrast to his tanned skin. "Ah, *scuzi.*" He pointed to the shiny gold nameplate on his broad chest. "I'm Officer Ricci. Detective DiNardo? He want me to come. To see … to *check* on you. From time to time. *Si?*"

Audrey smiled at him, because he seemed adorably eager to impress his boss. He couldn't have been on the force more than a year. For a moment, she wondered if she should invite him in for tea, for his trouble, but then she remembered Nick. "Oh, that's very nice of him, but you really don't have to …"

She stopped. This wasn't a check on her welfare, to make sure her heart was still ticking after the shock of seeing a dead body. It was to check to make sure she hadn't fled the country. The city.

Because she was, without a doubt, their number one suspect.

Her smile fell. "I'm here," she muttered. "Thanks."

She slammed the door and threw her weight against it. Nick came out and whimpered at her as she stared up at the water-stained ceiling that was badly in need of a new paint job. A paint job that would have to wait, especially with the police hanging around her door.

If she wanted to continue the renovations on the house, it was clear she'd have to prove her innocence first.

And she knew just where to start.

CHAPTER TWENTY ONE

The following morning, the second she heard the power saw going, she rocketed out of the house, excited to start her investigations. Audrey thought it a stroke of luck that any of the workers had shown up, especially since the police had put a moratorium on any renovation work at the scene.

Grabbing her trusty notepad, she rushed for the door, only to see Nick gazing hopefully at her from the foyer.

She held up a finger. "One second! Stay here. I promise I'll get you breakfast in a jiffy."

Opening the door just wide enough to squeeze through, she slipped out, nearly coming nose-to-chest with the officer from the day before. She would've forgotten his name if she hadn't nearly inhaled his nameplate.

"Officer Ricci, hi," she muttered. "You're up early."

Or maybe he'd slept under her window all night? That was a definite possibility, from the bleary look in his eyes. He flattened down a cowlick and stepped aside. "*Signorina. Buongiorno.*"

She looked to Nessa's house, where the saw was still trilling somewhere inside. But there were no vehicles around that looked as if they belonged to one of the crewmen. She looked at the officer. "I thought you guys ordered that no renovations were supposed to take place there until the investigation was over?"

His eyes went to the house. He cleared his throat, hesitating. "*Si.*" He lifted his radio and motioned to it. "I should see ..."

Audrey had taken one step closer to Piazza Due, but stopped when Nessa's unmistakable voice rang out over the racket. "For the love of all that's good and holy! How do you turn this thing off?"

The door swung open, and Nessa appeared in her running garb, decidedly more red-faced than she'd been yesterday. Her eyes narrowed at Audrey, and she opened her mouth, about to spit fire, when she caught sight of the young officer.

Her face softened. "Officer," she said in her sweetest voice, searching his nameplate. "Ricci?"

She proceeded to say something in Italian that had his Adam's apple bobbing up and down like a yo-yo. He nodded and followed her like a puppy on a leash. *"Si. Nessun problema."*

He followed her into the front door of her house. Audrey followed, too, just because she was curious as to the results of this massive renovation process, but Nessa blocked the way. "Sorry. I don't really like murderers in my houses. Do you know what you did to the resale value on this place? They find out there's been a murder here and I bet I never sell it. Even if it is a Nessa Goodroe property. I'll have to *eat* it."

Audrey gritted her teeth to keep from saying something she'd regret later. Calmly, she said, "I didn't murder a—"

At that moment, the sound of the saw cut off. Nessa clapped her hands together. "Oh, you've managed it! You're a dear! I couldn't tell which plug was which. They have like, twelve things in that strip."

While Nessa's back was turned, Audrey peered inside. The place was all pastels and wicker inside. Even with plastic drop-cloths on the ground, it looked more Golden Girls condo than crumbly nineteenth-century hovel.

Audrey quickly averted her eyes when Nessa turned back to her. Nessa raised her upper lip in a snarl of distaste, and shooed her with her hand like an insect. *Be off, peasant!*

Officer Ricci appeared, bowing humbly to her and blushing. Even though Audrey couldn't understand a word he said, she somehow knew he was babbling. He stepped outside just as a work truck with a ladder in the back pulled up.

Nessa groaned. "Oh, great. I called the construction company to come over and fix that blasted thing before Office Ricci stepped in." She focused her shooing hand on the truck and shouted, "I don't need you anymore! Go on your way!"

The man at the steering wheel didn't listen. He cut the engine and stepped out. He was a small, slight man, with shaggy dark hair and a bushy moustache. Audrey had the feeling she'd seen him before, at the worksite, a few days ago, but she was pretty certain he wasn't the guy that Ernesto had gotten into an argument with. That guy had been bigger, almost as beefy as Biceps himself.

One thing Audrey was sure of? This little guy never would've been able to push a big man like Ernesto to his death.

Nessa fisted her hands on her hips as he pointed to the door and said something in Italian. "Now?" She shook her head and said to

Audrey, "He has to pick up tools for another job. Another job, can you believe that? While my renovation is at a standstill, thanks to you."

The construction worker went inside to gather up the tools.

Nessa frowned. "Great. I just spent the night Cloroxing the place to get rid of all traces of sweaty Sicilian. Guess I'll have to do it again." She started to go inside and looked over at the officer. Her voice went saccharine. "Could I interest you in a cup of espresso, Officer Ricci?"

"*Grazie, si,*" he said, following her inside.

Well, didn't she know how to butter up the local law enforcement. Now, they all thought Nessa was a veritable saint, and the girl across the street from her, a devil. She sighed as the crewman came outside, one arm looped around a ladder, the other holding a folded workbench.

As he proceeded to drop them into the back of the truck, muttering something under his breath, Audrey approached him. "Excuse me. Sir? My name is Audrey and I live across the street. Do you speak English?"

He nodded warily.

"Do you think I can ask you a few—"

He was already backing away, looking as if he'd seen a ghost. "Oh, no. No no no. No more Americans. I've had enough, with that *diavola* in there. No more."

At least *someone* else saw through Nessa's shenanigans.

"I'm sorry. I understand. But I'm just looking into what happened to the foreman on the job. I feel terrible that he's dead," she said.

The man's eyes misted over. "Ernesto." He hung his head. "Yes. A better man never lived."

"Oh, so you were friends?"

He nodded. "We were the best. Grew up together. Had some good times." He clasped his heart. "I had to tell his poor Mariana about his passing."

Audrey raised an eyebrow, surprised. So Biceps actually had people who liked him? Interesting. "He had a wife?"

"Ex-wife. Oh, going on ten years. She lives in Chaos."

"Excuse me?"

"*Scuzi. Cavusu.* Chaos. Near Agrigento. On the shore."

He seemed pretty torn up, like a shell of the man who'd lugged the heavy equipment outside. Audrey didn't put it past him to collapse, weeping, right there in the street. She tugged on his sleeve. "Hey. Come in. I'm right here. I'll make you some tea. Like I said, I'm Audrey."

"Berto." He allowed her to drag him across the street, to her home. When they were in there, he sat down in one of the plastic chairs as she brewed the tea. Nick came over and sniffed at his work boots. "Oh, who's this?" he asked.

Audrey bit her tongue, hoping he wouldn't be a jerk and threaten to turn her in, like Ernesto had. "That's Nick. He was injured in someone's garden. I'm a v—"

"Ooh," he said, as Nick licked his palm. "What a cute thing."

Audrey relaxed. "Yes. I'm just nursing him back to health, and then I'll let him—"

"What's his name?"

She hesitated. "Nick."

"Ah." The animal jumped up onto the man's lap, and he let out a laugh of great surprise. Nick made himself comfortable as the man petted him, rolling on his side, purring like a kitten. "Very sweet."

Audrey brought over the teacups. "So … about Ernesto. I'm sure it must've been a shock to find out he died?"

He nodded. The second he lost interest in Nick and started to pour milk into his tea, Nick jumped from his lap and went off to the little nest of rags in the corner that Audrey had made for him. "Yes. Very shocking."

"You know the police think it could be murder."

He lifted the cup to his lips but did not respond.

"I've only been living here a couple weeks, but it seems like such a nice place. Who do you think could've done something like that?"

He shook his head. "None."

"You think he had any enemies? Like, someone else on his crew?"

"Ernesto? Nah."

Audrey sat down beside him and poured her own milk. She was hoping he'd mention the guy she'd seen fighting with Ernest, earlier. "Are you sure? Because a couple days ago, I thought he and someone on his crew got into a fight. The guy seemed really angry. Skull cap? Beard? He was wearing a T-shirt with a kind of dark flannel over it?"

Berto laughed. "You mean Peppe?" Audrey shrugged. "No. They're cousins. That's the thing with his crew. Grew up with most of them."

"But a couple days ago, I'm pretty sure I heard—"

"Nah. I know the fight you mean. Peppe's wife Carmen makes him *sfogliatelle* as a treat for lunch. Ernesto's fond of swiping them, as a joke, and eating them before Peppe can get his hands on them. We fight like cats and dogs, but it's all good and the end of the day. Murder? It'd never happen. Not with his people."

104

That wasn't helpful. Instead of getting a list of people who could've murdered Ernesto, now she had a list of people who *couldn't* have done it. "You're sure? I mean, humans do have an infinite ability to surprise. And I don't think the police think it was planned. Maybe he got into a fight, spur of the moment, and—"

"No. Besides, when it happened, most of the crew was in the south side of the city, with me. Setting up for our new job."

"Oh." Her eyes trailed to the notebook on the table, where she'd double-circled CREWMEN. There were no other possibilities on the paper, because she'd stupidly thought that for sure, this line of questioning would lead her somewhere. Suddenly, something occurred to her. "If everyone was setting up for a new job, why wasn't Ernesto there?"

"Ernesto went back to the American's house because ..." He stopped. His bushy eyebrows came together. "Come to think of it, I don't know why. He'd planned to meet us all at the new job. He must've wanted to check on something. We'd just plastered the walls. Maybe he wanted to check to make sure it set right."

"And that was normal for him?"

Berto hitched a shoulder. "Yeah. Sure." He studied Audrey carefully. "Now ... you're not police. Why do you care so much about Ernesto?"

"Oh ... I'm just an amateur detective, I guess. And I found the body, so I feel like I won't be able to rest until I know what happened to him. I'm sure you do, too, considering he was so well-liked around town."

"Ah. Well." He pushed away from the table. "Thank you for the tea. But I have to get back to the new job. *I'm* the foreman, now."

Audrey didn't bother to get up. She was still wondering where to go from here. It felt like a dead end.

Berto walked to the door and hesitated there. Then he turned. "Ernesto wasn't well-liked by everyone."

Audrey's ears perked up. "He wasn't?"

"No. He and his company, Fabri Fratelli, were starting to get a reputation in the town. He had a habit of bumping up material costs and overcharging people he didn't like. People he did like, too. A couple of times, he got called out on it, but he swept it under the rug. We tried to tell him to stop, that he had his head in the lion's jaws and one day he'd get it bitten off." He frowned. "When we heard the news, I think we all thought that was what happened."

Audrey's mouth opened, even before she could corral all the follow-up questions teeming in her head. Now, this was getting interesting. "Um … Really? So you think he might've gotten in a scuffle with a past customer?"

He shrugged. "Possible."

She shuffled to the edge of her seat and grabbed her pad. "Would you be able to tell me the names of the clients you did work for, in the past couple of months?"

"Well, let's see. There was old lady Bianco, and the new warehouse that we built near the church, and …" Audrey scribbled the names down as fast as he wrote, though none of the projects meant anything to her. It was only when he mentioned La Mela Verde that her ears pricked up.

"La Mela Verde? You mean that little café around the corner?"

He nodded. "The owner wanted to remove a wall and bump out the dining area. He was expecting a windfall with all the new foreigners coming to town. I know he and the owner got into a fight on the last day of the project."

"The owner … you mean G?" she asked, recalling the man with the infectious smile who'd asked her out on a tour. She'd gone by to see him yesterday, but he hadn't been in.

He shrugged. "I didn't think much of it. Seemed like every job we did lately, someone wasn't happy with it. But it was a pretty nasty one. The owner was refusing to pay, so I hear. Not sure if he ever did." He waved at her. "Take care, Audrey. Thanks for the tea."

Audrey smiled at him and watched him leave. As he did, she thought about G. He had an infectious smile, an easygoing personality, and didn't seem like the type to get angry about much. Then again, he'd asked her out. Considering all the other guys who expressed interest in her, she wouldn't put it past him to be a murderer.

But at least she had a lead. She scribbled his name down on the pad and furrowed her brow. G was a nice guy. At least, he had been, to her. But maybe he knew more than just how to make a great *ciambotta*.

CHAPTER TWENTY TWO

Now that she had a lead, Audrey wanted to waste no time in heading over to La Mela Verde. She closed Nick into the house before she left and said, "Be a good boy," like he was her actual pet.

The skies were threatening rain and thunder rumbled in the distance as she made her way down the block. Once again, it seemed like people on the street crossed to the other side to avoid having to talk to her. That had to be her imagination, as most of the people she was sure she'd never seen before. Unless gossip really did fly that fast?

A surprisingly cold wind blew, sneaking itself down her spine, ruffling the fringe on the café canopy and umbrellas and showing the undersides of the olive trees' leaves on the street. Audrey lifted the collar of her jacket to her neck as she passed by the empty café tables. Though it was just about lunchtime, no one would dare to eat outside with the coming storm. As she navigated through the tables, the wind blew over a chair and rattled the glass in the windowpanes.

She ducked inside as the first fat drops of rain began to fall.

G, who had been talking to a slim man in dark jeans and a traffic-cone-orange rain jacket at the end of the bar, greeted her warmly. "If it isn't *mi piccola Americana!*" he shouted from behind his counter, his voice booming over the din of the dining area.

If it had recently been renovated and enlarged, it was a good thing, because once again, every table was taken. She went to the table and sat down at a barstool. "Hi, G."

"Hi, yourself. You come in today for some more of my *ciambotta,* yes?"

She hadn't planned to, but when he mentioned it, her mouth started to water. She hadn't been shopping in a while, and the only food waiting for her at home was a little bit of stale Italian bread and some olive oil. She nodded. "Of course."

"Coming right up, for my favorite customer." He motioned toward the young man in the orange parka. "Talk to Liam, here. He's a foreigner, like you."

Slumped over his coffee like a man at a bar after a hard day's work, Liam eyed her cautiously from behind a pair of black-framed hipster glasses that were almost as dark as the circles around his eyes. He

107

looked like he hadn't shaved, or slept, in weeks. He didn't extend a hand to shake, just saluted briefly. "From London," he grumbled in a British accent.

"Nice to meet you. Did you buy a one-euro house, too?"

He winced, as if he'd rather not be reminded of the fact. "House is a bit of a stretch. More like a dumpster fire."

As sorry as she was to be a part of his misery, she was glad that not everyone was breezing through their renovations like Mason and Nessa had been. "What's going on?"

"What hasn't been going on? The thing's a bloody wreck, that's what," he snarled, in such a way that Audrey wished she hadn't asked. "Got here a fortnight ago. Thought I could get a jump on the renos before my boyfriend showed up, but I'm botching the thing left and right. Driving me barmy, it is. Yesterday, I went on the roof to repair a shingle and damned if I didn't fall straight through. Thing was rotted, termites, going to cost a bloody fortune to fix. I think I made a bad bargain."

Audrey's eyes widened as she watched G whirl toward the soup tureens, looking very much in his element as he effortlessly swept a bowl into his hand and ladled it in. "I'm so sorry. Are you a contractor?"

He shook his head. "Cal, my boyfriend, is, but he's finishing up a job. I rung him up and told him I want to call the thing. It isn't worth it, I told him."

Audrey patted her chest with sympathy. "I'm so sorry. You're not just going to give up, though, just like that? So easy?"

"Easy?" He scoffed and pushed his coffee cup away. "Not one bloody thing about this has been easy."

G gracefully slid the *ciambotta* under her nose with the standard hunk of crusty Italian bread. "But anything worth doing is hard! You don't give up! Right, Audrey? You push on. All part of the game of life."

Leave it to G to come in with the cheerleader routine. Audrey said, "That's right," and dipped her head to inhale from the dish. The smell of the stew made Audrey's mouth water even more. "Mmm."

He laughed. "Good, on a day like today, am I right?"

Audrey's eyes shifted to the windows, where the raindrops were now attacking the glass, creating a dark gray haze over everything outside. She shivered as she picked up her spoon. "Looks like I made it in just in time."

Liam threw a few dollars on the counter and grumbled, "Looks like I finished just at the wrong time," threw his hood over his head, and stalked outside.

Audrey watched him leave, head down, like he had the weight of the world on his shoulders. Talk about Johnny Raincloud. But she had to feel for the guy. She knew exactly what he was going through. In fact, she could *be* him, in another few days.

As if sensing her thoughts, G said, "How are your renovations going, little American?"

Audrey hated to admit that she hadn't even thought about renovations since poor Ernesto had met his end. "A little slow, truthfully. Hit a little roadblock. I need to get back into them."

He shot her a quizzical look. "That roadblock have anything to do with the murder you're accused of?"

Audrey had been blowing on a spoonful of the steaming stew, but she let it spill back into the bowl. He hadn't just said what she thought he said, had he? "Um, what?"

He smiled broadly. "Oh, you think I hadn't heard? News moves fast in this place."

She stared into her stew, her appetite suddenly gone. "What did you hear, exactly?"

"Ernesto Fabri finally got himself caught," he said, with so much enthusiasm, it was obvious there was no love lost there. "Someone got rid of the big spider. That's what he is, spinning webs … But I have a hard time believing why they'd think it was you, eh? Why would they, now? Just because you live where the body was found?"

She let out a big sigh. "It's more than that. I found the body, and I made the mistake of picking up his boot …" She cringed at the thought. "Forget it."

"Little thing like you, against a brick like that? Never."

He did have a point. "Unfortunately, the police don't see it that way. I guess they think it could be me because I was arguing with him the day before."

He laughed. "Is that it? If that's all they have to go on, he could've been murdered by half the town. Town's pretty small. All the locals know each other here."

She finally succeeded in getting a sip of the stew. Warm and delicious, the liquid coated her insides and made her feel instantly better. "I heard his construction company did some work for you, and you weren't happy?"

He nodded and pointed to the dining area. "I got an inheritance when my mama passed, so I put it into the business. Fabri Fratelli Construction's people made the room bigger. Was too small. But they cut the corners, used cheap materials, took twice as long as they promised. They were messy, too. No pride in their work."

Audrey recalled the heap of garbage and lumber that had been piled in front of her door. "I understand. That doesn't sound good."

"No. It wasn't. And then he told me he ran into unexpected expenses and wanted to charge me twice as much as he estimated. I told him to go to Hades. Chased him out of my place." He laughed at the memory. "I could be a suspect, too, eh? Along with everyone else. He's swindled half the people in this town, I'll bet you. *Bastardo.*"

"Really?" All these potential enemies. And the kicker of it was that somehow, *she'd* wound up being the police's prime suspect.

"*Si.* He's no good. Better off right where he is."

"Don't let the police catch you saying that. You will wind up on the suspect list with me. All I was doing was holding a boot."

He shrugged. "So be it. Let them come for me. I'm not scared of them."

Something occurred to Audrey right then. "Wait. You're saying the police haven't interviewed you yet?"

"No. But I'm ready, if they do." He flexed his muscles, which popped under his too-tight T-shirt. She could see the curve of them, even under his white apron. "I'll tell them just what they need to know."

"You did have a fight with him? You never paid him for his work?"

"No. I did not. And I never would've, either. Kept coming around, threatening me." He pounded his fist on the counter. "He was a bad one. It's no wonder he's dead."

She pressed her lips together, thinking. "I don't get it. I mean, you're the perfect suspect. You had a fight with him *and* you're big enough to have shoved him off the cliffside."

His voice grew quiet. "I'm sure there are many of us."

"Why wouldn't they at least come and ask you questions? That seems like shoddy policework to me."

"Maybe they're making their way through the list."

"Or maybe they've just been too busy hanging around my house, thinking *I* did it," she muttered bitterly. "Totally not fair, considering there are *real* suspects around."

His smile fell. He stared at her, and his voice took on an uncharacteristically serious tone. "What's this? You think I did it, Audrey?"

"Oh! No," she backpedaled. "Of course not. I just think they'd interview you first. You obviously have a lot of information they could find helpful."

Something in his countenance told her he didn't believe her. He pushed away from the counter and went to fill someone else's coffee cup, and after that, he didn't come back to talk to her, even when she was ready to pay. *Great. Now not only do most people in town think you are a murderer, but you've alienated pretty much the only friend you had in town. Nice going, Audrey.*

She'd planned to stay inside and wolf down second and third helpings of *ciambotta* until the rain stopped, but after a while, when she spun around on the stool, she realized that all of the eyes of the diners seemed to be on her.

Watching her. Judging her.

Just her imagination, again. Or maybe not …

Either way, she longed for the solitude of her little home. Throwing a few euros down on the counter, she slipped off the stool and stepped out into the driving rain.

As she walked through the puddles, she thought about G. Was it her, or had he gotten mighty defensive for no reason?

She wasn't paying attention, and wound up stepping in a puddle that swallowed and filled her entire shoe. She cringed as the cold water seeped into her sock.

Then she froze as every nerve ending stood at attention, and listened. She could've sworn she heard something other than the sound of the rain. Once again, she had the distinct feeling that she was being followed.

She whirled, raindrops drenching her face and blurring her vision. "Nick. Come out," she muttered, her words echoing through the empty street.

But this time, Nick didn't appear.

She searched up and down the street, wiping rain from her eyes, and then turned and hurried back to her house. By then, the magic of the *ciambotta* had worn off, and she was left shivering again.

CHAPTER TWENTY THREE

Audrey tilted her head as she crouched on her hands and knees in the bathroom. Straightened it. Tilted it again. Squinted.

That was weird.

Though she'd measured very precisely and used a level, she couldn't help feeling like the tiles on her new floor weren't even. In fact, they seemed to be going in a definite downward trajectory, just like her mood.

Ever since she'd moved in, she'd been longing for the feeling of nice travertine tile under her feet. Unlike the vast majority of jobs which gave her a bit of trepidation, this was one job she thought she'd have no trouble with. Growing up, she'd helped her father lay tile in over a dozen bathrooms and kitchens of the multimillion-dollar Back Bay mansions he renovated.

She smiled, thinking of the way she'd proudly wear her kid-sized toolbelt, following him around. She had to wonder if he was still out there somewhere, tiling bathrooms himself. If he missed having her as his little helper. He'd always loved his job and the houses he worked on, so much.

Of course, those had had the benefit of being ripped down to the studs and reconstructed from the ground up, and had nice clean angles and smooth walls.

She grabbed the level and checked it again. Her tiles were perfectly straight.

Which meant that the corner of the house was likely sinking. That probably wasn't good.

Sitting back on her haunches, she reached into her toolbox and picked up a screw, setting it on its side. Sure enough, it rolled right to that dark corner of the bathroom, behind the toilet.

It was fortunate she'd called to rent the tile cutter from the hardware store, as well as another box of tiles and some more grout. She was probably going to need the extra material, especially since she was pretty much guaranteed to make more mistakes.

"Whatever," she said, smoothing the grout for the next piece onto the floor with the trowel. As she did, Nick pranced by, trying to be smooth, cocking a curious eye her way. Her attention was caught by the fur of his tail. It wasn't poufy and red, as she was used to, but matted and gray. She stared at it. "What did you …?"

She looked around and noticed there were little gray footprints all over the kitchen floor.

"Ugh. No! You really stepped in it now," she groaned, scooping him into her arms. She brought him to the big porcelain kitchen sink and sat him there. "Don't fuss. I need to get that off you before it hardens, or else I'm going to have to cut it out."

He whined and scratched at her as she turned on the water. She tried to scrub him, but he flailed his limbs and tail, body alternating rapidly between boneless and board-stiff, spraying water everywhere and carrying on like she was torturing him. "Calm down!" she shouted at him as he swiped at her wrist. "Ouch!"

She pulled away and glared at the four straight lines on the pale, tender skin of her inner wrist. He took that as his moment to escape, his tail splashing her face and chest with a small wave of water as he scampered out of the sink, to the counter, and finally to the floor. The floor around the sink was soaked, and Audrey's clothes couldn't have been wetter if she'd dove into the nearest lake.

"Ugh. Great," she said. Water dripped off the end of her nose as she inspected her wrist. The wound wasn't deep, but nevertheless, it began to bubble with blood.

She went to reach for her medical bag when someone rapped lightly on the door.

That was probably Luca, from the hardware store. "Come in!"

He didn't.

He probably couldn't hear her, or maybe it was a Sicilian custom not to go in unless the door was opened for you. Or maybe he was just being polite. She grabbed a couple of napkins from the table and clamped them over the wound as she went to the foyer.

Blood seeped through it almost immediately, though, pouring between her fingers and coating her hand. Funny how something that barely stung could bleed so much. *Gross. I hope I don't need stitches. Thanks, Nick.*

"Hi," she said as she pulled open the door to see Luca standing there with his trusty cart nearby, much of his face hidden by a slouchy hoodie. She peered out, cautiously looking both ways. No Officer Ricci, at least. He hadn't come to "check" on her since that morning. It was still raining outside, and Luca looked vaguely miserable to be out in the chilly air.

Though he did a double take when he saw her looking just as much like a drowned rat as he was, he didn't say anything. His eyes swept to her bloody hands. He took a step back, alarmed.

"Sorry." She looked down. Wow, how much could one little wound bleed? It mixed with the water she'd been doused in, and now it was all over the front of her white T-shirt. "Had a little mishap. With my ..." She stopped short of saying *pet,* even though it was on the tip of her tongue, on the off chance that Luca was as stringent about animal control laws in the city as Ernesto had been.

Quickly averting his eyes, he lifted the box of tile from the cart and slid it onto the foyer floor. He placed the tile cutter beside it, and the tub of grout atop it.

She dabbed at the wound as she inspected the delivery. The box was unmarked; she'd have to open it to make sure the tile was the right color. "Great. Thank you. What's the damage?"

He reached into his pocket and pulled out a crumpled slip of paper, his hands shaking. Poor kid must be freezing. "Two-twenty."

She tried not to let on that it was twice as much as she was hoping he'd say. Everything so far with this renovation had a price tag that was reliably double what she'd been hoping, and now that little nest egg of hers was almost microscopic. "Let me go get my purse so I can pay you," she said as brightly as she could to disguise her woes. "Want to come in? I can make you some tea. You look chilled to the bone."

He shook his head adamantly.

Strange, she thought as she grabbed her purse off the kitchen table. She didn't have a pair of scissors so she grabbed the nearest knife, a butcher's knife with a wide, silver blade. *He was such a chatterbox the other day. A real ladies' man.*

Luckily, she had enough euros this time to pay in cash, plus provide a little tip for his delivery. When she got to the door, though, Luca was facing the house across the street, staring intently at it and the police tape that had been stretched across the gate to the back of the house. No doubt, he'd heard the news.

The moment she appeared in the doorway again, he jumped up like a Jack in the Box and his Adam's apple bobbed. He stared at the knife. She handed the bills over to him with her blood-sticky fingers, which he took quickly, murmuring a *Grazie.*

She reached down to open the box with the knife. "Let me just check ..." She stopped when she realized she was alone. He was halfway down the street before she could even say *Ciao.*

Odd, she thought, but only for a split second. Because at that moment, realization crept in.

For a second she thought to call him back to explain to him, but by then, he and his squeaky-wheeled cart were long gone. Besides, the tile was the correct, off-white color she'd ordered.

Great. Luca thinks you're a mass murderer. Now you're really on the good side of the owners of the hardware store, Aud. You might as well consider wallpapering your house in leaves and making your own tools out of branches and recycling. That is, before they run you out of town with pitchforks and shovels.

Not that she was even *allowed* to leave town. But maybe they'd make an exception for a crazy person like her.

As she was about to close the door, Nessa appeared in her own doorway across the narrow street. Doing everything possible not to look Audrey's way, she stuck a hand out to check for rain. Satisfied, she started to fasten her earbuds into her ears, when she finally looked at Audrey.

"Just so you know," she called in a sing-song voice. "You're going to get in a lot of trouble if anyone finds out you're harboring a wild animal."

Audrey's jaw dropped. So the girl who seemed oblivious to her in general only noticed her when she was doing something potentially illegal. Check.

"What did it do?" She motioned to her arm. "Scratch you? Bite you? Figures. They call them *wild* animals for a reason. Better get yourself some rabies shots."

"He just got overexcited. He doesn't have rabies. I should know. I'm a v—"

"Whatever," she muttered. "Just don't be snooping around my place anymore, okay? I saw that construction worker leaving your house. I don't know what you think you're doing, but these are *my* designs. I worked hard on them. So just butt out of my business. I don't want to have to sic my team of lawyers on you."

She took off on her run in her skimpy running shorts and bra top before Audrey could even think to respond. Her designs? Snooping around her place? There was so much wrong with that, Audrey couldn't even begin to process it.

Audrey watched her go, her ponytail swishing out behind her, and realized her nose was wrinkled in a scowl. *She is not a nice person. In fact, she's a nightmare. If Luca should be scared of anyone, it's her.*

115

Audrey closed the door and caught Nick staring up at her, and was that an apologetic look on his face?

"I don't care, fox. You're in the doghouse," she said, even though she'd already started to soften to him. She sat down on a kitchen chair and inspected the wound. The flow of blood had stopped. She applied antibiotic and wrapped her wrist in gauze, then taped it up.

Was Nessa really more concerned about someone stealing her home designs than about the fact that someone had lost his life on her property?

Must've been nice, being able to go on a run and enjoy life despite that. Audrey didn't have the luxury of simply blocking it out of her mind and forgetting. She wasn't wired that way. In fact, ever since it'd happened, it'd never left her mind, even for a second. When she closed her eyes, it was Ernesto's body she saw, lying in a pool of blood at the bottom of the cliff.

One event, and her life had been turned completely upside down. And she hadn't even committed the crime. She'd just been accused of it, thanks to Nessa.

She grabbed paper towels and slipped to the ground to clean up the small lake in her kitchen, wishing she could be more like Nessa, completely oblivious, like absolutely nothing had happened. Nessa, who had effectively turned all suspicion on the wrong person, leaving the real culprit to get off scot-free. Would she even feel guilty if Audrey was proven innocent? Or was she so above it all that she really only cared for herself?

I hope Ernesto overcharged her for her materials before he was killed. Grossly overcharged her.

Something tickled at the back of Audrey's mind. She froze.

If Ernesto *had* overcharged her, and Nessa had found out about it, well, that would be motive for her to commit murder, too. Just like G said. *Half the town has a reason to murder him.*

Audrey straightened as a thought occurred to her. What better way to take suspicion off oneself than by throwing it on someone else?

Nessa had a motive. But did she have an alibi?

Kind of. Audrey had seen her go for a run.

It was not watertight, though. Nessa had been in the area. It wouldn't have taken long to commit a murder … seconds at most. What had she been doing before Audrey saw her? Audrey strained to remember. Had she just come from her house, or had she come from the backyard?

And yes, Nessa had *said* she went for a jog, and had come back because she'd forgotten her sunglasses.

Or had she?

Maybe she'd invented the ruse of going for her run just so she could return at the right moment to throw the blame on Audrey.

Audrey shivered as the thought planted itself in her mind.

Nessa's not a nice person, but ... is she a murderer?

CHAPTER TWENTY FOUR

"Hey. Look at you. Still walking among the free."

Audrey hadn't meant to walk past Mason's door, but after Nessa's comments and Luca's behavior toward her, not to mention an altogether frustrating experience with her travertine tile, she needed to get away. She didn't mind the last downpour because there was no one out there to give her the stink-eye. But now that the rain was over and the day was just overcast, as her wet hair hung in ropes on her face, and her waterlogged clothes sagged on her body, she had to admit she felt self-conscious.

Why did Mason always have to look so effortlessly good? His clothes were wrinkled like he'd just rolled out of bed, he hadn't shaved, probably hadn't showered, and there were paint splotches on his arms. The things that would serve to make a woman look like crud actually enhanced his image.

And really, she didn't have time for perfect, problem-free people right now.

She muttered a response and tried to walk past him, but he jumped from his front stoop, where he'd been enjoying a beer, and blocked her way. "Is it really that bad?"

She looked down at the remaining puddles on the ground. "It's not bad. I'm fine. I'm just not in the mood for talk."

"Oh, yeah? Does this have to do with a certain crime you didn't commit?"

He said it with a lilt in his voice, like it was all a joke.

"Obviously. And it's not funny."

"Never said it was."

"You implied it." She tilted her chin back to look into his eyes, and wished she hadn't. He had her dangerously close to giggling moronically again. Why couldn't he allow her time to mope?

"Why don't you come in, take a load off, have a beer with me?" He held up a dark bottle, as if trying to tempt a dog with a treat. "I've got Minchia Tosta. Sicilian beer. It's *delicious*."

There it was, the giggle. She'd never been one for beer but she realized that even though he was an animal-hater, his eyes made it

118

pretty hard to say no. Nick would be so disappointed in her. "All right. Just one."

"Good." He turned to go back into the house, and as she trailed in behind him, trying to ignore how well he filled out those jeans, he added, "Then I can borrow you for a project."

She groaned. "What do you need now? Another animal for me to rescue?"

"No, nothing like that. Hey," he said, looking back at her. "What happened to your arm?"

"Don't ask."

"I think I already did."

"All right. Then I won't answer."

Instead of leading her into his kitchen, he brought her to the back of the house, where there was a yellow living room that looked like something out of *Better Homes*. It was probably as big as her entire Boston apartment, and it had floor-to-ceiling greenhouse windows that looked out onto the patio. Despite the clouds in the sky, the room was sunny and bright and cheerful—and *exactly* what she'd envisioned when she'd planned to move to Sicily, all those weeks ago. Audrey sighed wistfully.

He snapped his fingers at her again, like she was a dog. "Hello? Focus here."

For someone who hated animals, he had no trouble treating people like them. She crossed her arms and went to him at a stepstool, noticing a couple of floating shelves on the ground. He picked up one and held it against the wall.

"Yeah, so if you can just hold this for me, right about ... here ..." He squinted, making sure it was level. "Then I can get this show on the road."

"Fine." She held it for him as he said, "Don't move it!"

"I'm not!"

He held up a drill. "Yes you are." He placed it again, in exactly the place she'd been holding it. "There. Right there. Don't move."

She groaned. The drill whirred. The nails drove into the plaster.

"All right. Good. You can let go."

She did and relaxed her arm. "That was heavy. You have Luca from the hardware store deliver?"

"No. I have my own car. I get my own supplies." He motioned to a small stack of them that Audrey hadn't seen before. "Now the next one."

"Ugh. How many of these are you putting up?"

119

"Three more."

"Three? Where's my beer?"

"In a second. I need to get these up," he said, grabbing ahold of the next shelf. "Otherwise I have nowhere to put my books."

She snorted. "You can read?"

"Funny." He didn't laugh.

Eventually, she wound up on the sectional, a soft, buttery yellow monstrosity that was so much more wonderful than her lumpy mattress at her place. When she collapsed in it, she didn't want to get up. It'd been a long time since she'd lain in actual, nice furniture. She wondered if he'd get the wrong idea if she asked to sleep there. "Where'd you get this?"

He popped the top on his beer and sat in a modern wingback, propping his work boots on a reclaimed-wood coffee table. "All this was actually in the place when I moved in. I struck the jackpot. Just had it cleaned."

She groaned. "How fortunate for you," she said through her teeth, trying to squelch her envy.

"So ... how are the police getting on with their investigation?"

Audrey took a sip of her beer. It was bitter, but she didn't mind the taste now. She shrugged. "They haven't come to ask me any questions since it happened. But they do send an officer by every so often to check on me. Make sure I haven't skipped town. So I guess they really haven't made much headway. They're probably too busy building their case against me to go out and find the real killer."

"Okay ... but if you didn't do it, someone else did. Who?"

She shrugged. "I heard he had a big reputation for overcharging his clients, so maybe one of them."

He scratched his chin. "What happened that morning? Didn't you see anyone around there before you found him?"

"I saw Nessa. My neighbor. The American who lives at the place where the body was found. He was working for her."

"You mean the hot girl?"

Of course he'd taken notice of Nessa. She was probably used to getting attention, just like him. Two peas in a pod. "Right. She said she was going for a run, but she could've argued with him and pushed him over. I don't know."

He shook his head definitively. "Nah."

Audrey frowned at him. Nessa was her main suspect. "Why not?"

"Because she's hot. She doesn't look like the murdering type."

Audrey rolled her eyes. "Oh, right. Of course. What we're really looking for is the murdering type. Black cloak? Shifty eyes? Maybe a ski mask?"

Ignoring her, he drained the rest of his bottle, thinking. "And what about the other guys that work on the crew? It could've been one of—"

"I don't think so. I spoke to one of them. He said they're like family. And most of them were at another site. But this guy, Ernesto Fabri, had a lot of enemies, supposedly. It was well-known that he liked to bilk his customers by overcharging them for materials," Audrey explained. "So my thought is that maybe Nessa found out, and there was a fight, and she accidentally pushed—"

"Nah," he said again.

"Oh, right. I forgot. She's too hot to do such a horrible thing."

He nodded as if it made absolute sense. She picked up a pillow and made like she was about to launch it at him.

He held up his hand in defense. "Come on. No, what I mean is that she's rich, right? She doesn't exactly strike me as the type to even notice if she'd been overcharged."

Audrey nodded. He had a point there, even if he was a total ass. Not only was Nessa probably wealthy enough that being gypped out of a few dollars wouldn't have even registered in her massive bank account, she was tiny, too. She'd have a hell of a time pushing a giant guy like Fabri over a cliff. "I guess. But she was there. No one else was. At least, no one I saw."

"All right, but he had a lot of enemies. Someone knew he was there, and whether they went there to talk to him, or to kill him, it doesn't matter. So someone who knew he'd be there?"

"Well, according to his crewman, he was supposed to be at another site but he went to Nessa's house instead. Maybe to check on something. So I don't think it was planned, because he really wasn't supposed to be there in the first place. All I know is that Nessa was there. And maybe she didn't shove him. Maybe he just fell on his own, somehow, and the sign of struggle was her trying to help him back up. But then, why wouldn't she say that? Ugh! None of this makes sense."

"Right. It could have nothing to do with the renovations," Mason said. "Maybe it was meant to look like that."

Audrey took a swig of her beer. "Oh, right, so they could frame poor, innocent, hot Nessa?"

He nodded. "Dang shame."

She scowled at him. He may have dismissed Nessa, but she wasn't going to let her off the hook so easily. After all, she was the only suspect she had. And, if she was being honest, a little part of her *wanted* Nessa to be guilty, after what she'd done to her, thrusting her to the top of the suspect list.

"If only you were that concerned about *my* being framed," she muttered. "You realize it's mostly because of Nessa that the police even suspect me at all?"

Mason shrugged. "Like I said, a shame."

"So I can't just sit back and let them pile up evidence on me. I have to do something." She pounded the bottle on her thigh, and it began to bubble over, dripping on her already wet jeans. She ran a finger up the side of the bottle and sucked on it. "I guess I just don't know where to start."

He rubbed the stubble on his jaw. "If I were you, I'd start with the victim. Find out what you can about him. Check his social media, his business website, stuff like that. Make connections. One of those connections could lead you right where you're wanting to go."

She nodded thoughtfully. That made total sense. She could easily hit up Google, and without even setting foot outside. Why hadn't she thought of that before?

"Wow, Mason. I think that may be the first smart thing you've ever said to me."

He let out a bitter laugh. "You're hilarious."

She sipped her beer. "Thanks."

"But you better be careful, girl. You don't want to get that pretty nose of yours too close to the truth. Could get bitten off."

He stared at her in an intense way, and it seemed like this would be the moment in a murder mystery movie where the foreboding organ music would swell up and leave the audience chilled.

But Audrey only giggled again. *He called me pretty. Well, my nose, at least.*

From the way he looked at her, he must've been used to that kind of reaction. "Seriously. I know you want to clear your name, but if that person killed once, there's not much that'd stop him from killing again."

*

That night, Audrey fell down a rabbit hole.

Vaguely aware that it was the internet that had gotten her into this trouble in the first place—because it was that stupid ad on her Facebook feed that had led her to Mussomeli—she snuggled under the covers of her bed and let her thumbs get their exercise, typing in, *Ernesto Fabri, Mussomeli.*

There were a number of hits, including photographs of the same cigar-sucking, massive-biceped guy, in younger days, before the giant pot belly and the receding hairline. The first website was for Fabri Fratelli Construction.

She clicked on it and was dismayed to find out the entire thing was in Italian. Of course. She scrolled to the bottom, though, and found what looked to be the address and phone number. Grabbing her pad, she scribbled that information down, wondering if she'd have the guts to snoop around there and ask questions.

As she finished, Mason's words came back to her: *If a person killed once, there's not much that'd stop him from killing again.*

A shiver snaked down her spine. She'd just shoved the willies away when a giant red furball dropped in her lap.

She jumped, not as high as last time. "Nick, can you stop floating around the place like the face of death? Can't you make a little noise so you don't scare me?"

Unconcerned, he circled around her bed, scanning for the most comfortable spot, and found it at her elbow. He plopped himself down, head on her pillow, and licked at his paw.

"Fine. Whatever. This is your bed. I just borrow it." She went back to the Google results and noticed a search result for *FINDANYONEANYWHERE.com.* She knew it was clickbait, but she opened it anyway. It had a listing for Ernesto Fabri in Mussomeli, Sicily, with some of the numbers and important data concealed unless the user purchased a paid report. Audrey wasn't stupid or desperate enough to do that; besides, the free listing gave her enough information:

Fabri, Ernesto R. Age: 49, Tomasino di Bartolo ***, Mussomeli, Sicily, IT. **bri@fabri.com. Possible Relations: Mariana (De Mauro) Fabri (39). Eduardo Fabri (68) Giuseppe Fabri (46). THIS INDIVIDUAL MAY HAVE A CRIMINAL RECORD. CLICK HERE TO ORDER DETAILED REPORT.

Right. Berto had said that Mariana Fabri was the ex-wife, living in Agrigento.

She clicked out of it and typed in *Mariana Fabri, Agrigento.*

Immediately she came up with a bunch of hits, but the second she saw the images of a blonde woman in a tight-fitting, cleavage-revealing shirt and a tan, she knew she'd found the right woman. She scanned through the pictures and finally found one of her with a man who looked like Ernesto, from about a decade ago. He had one of his big biceps wrapped possessively around her neck.

Bingo.

It turned out that Mariana Fabri was the classic over-sharer. She was active on just about every social media platform out there, especially Facebook, and her profile was completely public. She had almost the limit of five thousand friends, and updated about once an hour, with a funny meme or a photograph of herself.

A *lot* of photographs of herself.

Apparently, since her split from Ernesto, she'd gone through a second youth. Audrey scanned through selfie after selfie of the woman, feeling almost embarrassed with how little she was wearing. They were mostly bikini shots, either her posing in the arms of random men, or holding some fruity cocktail and looking a little bleary in the eyes. Her hair had gradually gotten longer and lighter, too—now it was white blonde. No posts about children. It was all about *her*—what beach she was jetsetting to for a party, what pseudo-celebrities she was living it up with, what fabulous concert she'd attended.

Audrey felt a sick feeling plant itself in her gut as she scrolled. Sure, Mariana had made it all public, inviting the scrutiny, but Audrey couldn't help feeling like she was intruding. Stalking.

She stopped when she came to a memory of a picture that had been taken fifteen years before. A much younger Mariana, dressed as a blushing bride, complete with veil and too-much-tulle white dress, with a much trimmer and more attractive Ernesto, toasting their wedding. Over the picture, Mariana had written a caption, with a laughing emoticon.

Audrey eagerly pushed the *Read Translation* button.

It said, *"Worst day of my life!"*

Interesting. She clicked on the comments. There were many from her male admirers, all in Italian.

She clicked on the translation of one, that said, *Thank goodness for divorce!*

Mariana had replied, *Not yet. I ask for one every year and he says no. Bastard.*

Audrey stared at the words so long that they blurred together. There it was, a big fat motive. So if he had a life insurance policy, and he was killed, she'd be the beneficiary. Not to mention that she'd get him out of the way so she could remarry.

Her eyes went to the woman. No cloak, no mask … heck, this woman clearly loved to bare everything. *Everything*. Was *she* the murdering type?

Audrey dropped her phone and tilted her head to the ceiling, thinking. No, Mariana probably had just as much strength as Nessa did, as Audrey did, and probably couldn't have pushed a man like Fabri. But anything was possible. Maybe there was a fight, and he'd lost his balance.

In that case, Nessa wasn't off the hook. Neither was Mariana.

Her thoughts ran in circles, but they kept coming back to the same conclusion: She *had* to talk to this woman. There was no way around it.

No, Audrey wasn't allowed to leave town.

But what the police didn't know wouldn't hurt them. It'd only hurt her … if she got caught.

CHAPTER TWENTY FIVE

The next morning, before she even slid out of bed, she grabbed her phone and called Mason.

He answered, groaning. "You realize it's barely seven in the morning?"

She ignored his complaining. "You said you had a car?"

"Yeah ..."

"Can I borrow it?"

Now he seemed more awake. "What do you need a car for?"

She was a woman with a plan. She'd spent the entire sleepless night ruminating. When she finally did fall asleep, well after three in the morning, she had dreams of leading the police on a car chase through the mountains of Sicily, only to plunge off a cliff into the same Mediterranean Sea she'd ogled with desire from the subway back in Boston. A fitting ending to her life.

But now, she had a nagging need to escape. Never before had she felt it so bad. It was even worse than the impulse that had brought her all the way from America. That one was about preserving her sanity. This one felt like a matter of life or death.

"I want to go to Agrigento. It's a town on the coast. Not far from here. Fabri's wife lives there. I think she might be able to help me clear up a little bit on his past."

A pause. "So all my warnings did no good, I see."

"No, listen. She has a motive to kill him because he never granted her a divorce, and she *clearly* wanted to move on. She'd asked him a bunch of times, and he said no."

"How do you know this?"

"It's amazing the things people post on Facebook."

"Facebook post nothing. She's a woman. That guy was a rock. She'd have a hard time—"

"Right, but he could have slipped during a fight. I don't know. I won't know unless I ask. And Agrigento isn't far away, so there's a chance—"

"That you're driving to the coast to meet with a murderer and I'll never see you—or my car—again? So, yeah, as to whether you can borrow my car? I'd say that's a big no."

"Come on. What am I supposed to do? Sit back and let them conduct the investigation themselves?"

"Well … yes. Last thing I heard, that was their job. Not yours."

"*No.* I told you. If I do that, next thing I know, they'll be knocking on my door with an arrest warrant. I need to be proactive."

"No. You need to sit tight. Mind your own business. Acting strange is only going to make you look more suspicious."

Audrey went to the picture window and threw it open. She peered out onto the street. No Officer Ricci, surprisingly. She hadn't seen him since yesterday, when he stopped by on his reconnaissance mission, but that didn't mean he wouldn't be around again, camping out outside her place. "I *was* minding my own business. That got me where I am today."

There was a short pause. Finally, he sighed. "Fine. It's the blue Fiat in front of my house. I'll leave the keys in the ignition."

Okay, so, distancing yourself from the crazy neighbor so you're not implicated. Got it. She didn't bother to question it. He'd said yes. That was enough. "Thanks. I'll be there in fifteen."

"Be careful, Boston."

She hung up and decided to forgo the shower, quickly dressing and grabbing an apple from the kitchen. Once again, she tripped over Nick as she reached for the door. "Oh. Um …" She reversed direction and filled a cereal bowl with a scoop of dog kibble and a slice of the apple. "That should keep you. Don't go anywhere."

She closed the door and was just about to head toward Mason's house and take a bite of her apple when she noticed Officer Ricci coming toward her.

Her gut dropped.

"*Ciao,*" he said, giving her a wave. There was a suspicious lilt in his voice that Audrey didn't like. Or maybe that was just her imagination? "You're up early. Where are you headed?"

"To visit a friend," she said, lips tight. "That's all."

She turned away from him so that he couldn't detect the lie on her face, then feeling guilty, held up her hand for a wave.

"See you later!"

When she rounded the corner, she realized her heart was beating out of her chest. She clamped a hand over it and picked up the pace.

Mason's powder blue Fiat was parked almost directly in front of his home, but Mason was nowhere in sight. Audrey had pegged Mason as more of a pick-up truck, gun-fanatic, country-music-loving Southern boy, and this car was almost the exact antithesis of that. It was so tiny that the walls closed in on Audrey as she slid into the seat, and she wasn't exactly big. Mason probably had trouble fitting all of his six feet of perfection behind the wheel.

Of course, a pick-up truck probably couldn't manage the narrow streets very well. The car was made for a city like Mussomeli.

She found the key already in the ignition, a metal keychain dangling against her knee. The car sputtered to life as she twisted the key, checking in her rearview mirror, expecting Officer Ricci to show up, banging a bully stick against his palm and shaking his fist like a Keystone Cop.

But no, there was no one on the street at all.

No witnesses to notice her escape.

"I'm crazy," she whispered to herself, peering at a street sign up ahead. It was an inverted triangle. No clue what that meant. Luckily, Sicilians drove on the right side of the road, just like Americans, or else she probably would've called it a day and gone back home, tail between her legs, and waited to be arrested.

Then she looked down and realized something.

The car was a manual.

Driving an automatic car was hard enough, considering she hadn't owned one at all in Boston. Never had the need to, with the T. She'd learned the basics on how to drive a manual on a whim about a decade ago, from one of Brina's boyfriends, while he was killing time waiting for Brina to get ready for a date.

Gingerly, she stepped on the gas, and the car lurched forward, gears grinding. She winced. "Mason, I apologize to you in advance if I leave your transmission in the middle of the road."

She threw the shifter back and inched away from the curb.

Audrey didn't breathe the entire trip down Mason's street. She wrapped her white-knuckled fingers around the steering wheel and said silent prayers the entire time. But when she turned onto the main drag, even though she was soon to be an "outlaw," she could breathe a little easier. She eventually got the hang of shifting, too, and the gears didn't grind nearly as much, even on the many hills.

She rolled down the windows and let the warm summer air roll through cabin, taking big mouthfuls of it. It felt good to be free.

"I can do this," she said to herself with a smile as she checked her phone in the cup holder beside her.

Agrigento, only about twenty-eight more miles away. Luckily, Mariana Fabri, the over-sharer on social media, was well spread out all over the internet. It only took a quick Google search to find her address, which was what she punched into her GPS.

She reached over to turn on some music but the only thing that came through was some terrible Italian pop that sounded like an animal wailing in pain. She flipped it off and reached into the other cup holder for her forgotten apple half, her breakfast, which she was sure would now be mostly brown goo.

But it was gone.

She reached blindly into the passenger's side floor, feeling around the seat for the missing fruit. Instead, her hand came in contact with something furry and warm.

The second she touched it, it flinched.

"Ack!" she screamed, nearly letting go of the wheel as Nick jumped out at her, sitting himself on the passenger seat and making himself at home, already half-done with her breakfast. As he munched, he peered, unconcerned, over the dashboard as she veered sharply to the right and nearly hit a street sign.

She corrected just in time, then came to a stop at something she was pretty sure was a stop sign.

There were no cars behind her, so she turned to him, frowning. "Really?"

He finished the rest of the apple—even the core—and licked his paws.

"Nice. How did you even get out here?"

Behind her, a car beeped.

She jumped and pressed on the gas, heading toward the edge of town.

"You play nice and innocent," she muttered to him, "but deep down, you're a sneaky one." All she could think was that there must be a hole somewhere that he was escaping through. She didn't put it past her place to have plenty of holes in it. It was like the Swiss cheese of homes.

She was about to berate him on eating her breakfast when a siren sounded behind her.

Then she *really* jumped, so high the top of her head nearly scraped the car's roof. Peering in the rearview mirror, she saw the red flashing lights. She navigated over to the side of the road, biting her lip. As she did, she realized she was about a stone's throw from a sign that said, *Partiamo ora da Mussomeli,* which she hoped meant that she was still within the city limits.

Her heart sped up as she tilted her head to look in the side-view mirror and saw Officer Ricci stepping toward her on the dusty shoulder of the road. Perfect. She was totally screwed.

Breathing hard, she threw her head back against the headrest and tried to calm herself. That was when Nick lounged across the seat and rested his head on her lap.

Oh. She'd forgotten about him.

No. *Now* she was totally screwed.

She shoved the fox off her lap and powered down the window. "Hello, Officer!" she said brightly, waving. "Nice day for a drive, huh?"

Who was this girl? It didn't even sound like her own voice. Somehow, even though she wanted to throw up, she'd actually managed to sound halfway normal. Was that what being suspected of murder did to a person? Now that she was a hardened criminal, she could lie like that, with the drop of a hat? She scared herself.

Officer Ricci crossed his arms. "Where were you headed?"

He no longer sounded friendly. In fact, he sounded downright *pissed*.

"Um... just like I said. On a drive, to check out the city," she said, shielding her eyes from the sun and squinting into the distance. "Though I think I might've gotten a little lost."

"I think so." His face was stone. "I thought you said you were going to visit a friend?"

She gritted her teeth. She had said that. "Yes! Right!" she hedged. "Checking out the city, visiting friends in town, it's all good."

"You were almost *outside* of town."

She nodded. "I just noticed the sign. Whoops. Good thing you stopped me."

"You know, Detective DiNardo won't be happy. I could have you arrested."

Before she could answer, Nick made a little squeaking noise that almost sounded like an "uh-oh." Officer Ricci shifted slightly, peered in the back seat, and shook his head.

"And that's not legal. Your neighbor reported that you might be harboring a wild animal."

My neighbor. Nessa, of course. She'd wormed her way right into Officer Ricci's heart. What other lies had she been feeding him? "Yes, but I'm a veterinarian and—"

"Do you have a license?"

Well, he had her there. She shook her head.

He rubbed his temple tiredly. "All right. I'll pretend I never saw you if you turn around right now and go back home. *And* if you release that animal out into the wild immediately. You understand?"

She did. She knew she had to. She nodded, but Nick, not understanding any of this, wormed his way under her arm and sat in her lap, panting like her pet. How adorable. Her heart twisted.

But Officer Ricci clearly wasn't under the same spell. "Audrey? Are you listening?"

She sighed. "Yes. Fine. Thank you, Officer. I appreciate your help." She stared ahead, into the wide, open valley, which was now completely off-limits to her. It was like she'd trekked a thousand miles only to have the door or her destination slammed in her face.

Somewhere out there was Mariana Fabri. A possible murderer.

Somewhere out there were answers. She was sure of it.

"You know," she blurted suddenly, still unable to take her eyes off the road she so desperately wanted to travel. "Ernesto Fabri, the foreman, had a wife, supposedly, who he refused to divorce. She hated him for that reason. So if there was any, I don't know, life insurance on him, she'd be a rich woman."

He stared at her, his mouth a straight line.

"Just some food for thought!" she said brightly. It didn't hurt to plant the seed. "I'm sure you've heard of plenty of disgruntled wives staging their husbands' deaths by making it look like an on-the-job accident? Especially for the insurance money?"

"Audrey," he mumbled, shaking his head. "Detective DiNardo and I have already investigated Mariana Fabri."

She stiffened and slinked into the seat. Well, she hadn't expected that little turn of events. "You have?"

"Yes. We went out there yesterday. The woman's clean. She'd had a dinner party the night before, and over a dozen people saw her at her home the following morning. There's no possible way she could've done it."

Audrey just stared, speechless. If Mariana Fabri hadn't done it, then …

Then that meant she was right back at square one.

He pointed. "If you make a U here, keep following this road, you'll wind up at the center of town," he said, which of course, she already knew.

"Thanks," she muttered.

But what she really thought was, *I am never going to be allowed to leave this town again.*

CHAPTER TWENTY SIX

Mason was outside, installing a new light fixture on the front stoop, when she returned, no more than thirty minutes after she'd embarked on her name-clearing journey. When she pulled the car to a grinding halt outside his house, he eyed her, his swimming-pool blue eyes wide with concern, which almost made her feel better.

Until she stepped out of the little car, came around it, and realized he hadn't been looking at her. No, he was more concerned about the stupid car. He reached over and wiped some imaginary dust off the Fiat's side mirror.

"Watch it, girl. Who taught you how to drive a stick?"

She sighed and held out the keys. "Some random guy, kind of like you."

He opened his palm, and she dropped them in. He immediately opened the passenger side door and looked around, sat inside, then actually *petted* the dashboard.

"It was a big bust. Thanks for asking," she muttered, heading for her house. "Come on, Nick."

"Hey, wait—" He stopped short. "Who's ..."

Just then, Nick scampered from the back seat, onto his lap, and hopped out the door. Mason let out an almost girlish shriek.

"What the ... was that *thing* in my car?"

"Yep." Right now, she had more important things to worry about than offending pretty boy.

He let out a groan. "Frig. There's hair everywhere. And little freaking paw prints!"

She whirled on him. "Listen, you car-obsessed freak. I'm a little busy dealing with other things now, so pardon me if I don't offer to vacuum your upholstery."

She wasn't expecting the effect her words had on him. He actually took a step backward, like he might be scared of her. Maybe she didn't know her own strength.

He shrugged and slammed the door. "I'm not obsessed. I just bought the dang thing. It's not new, but it's new to me, and I'd like it to stay that way."

She sighed. She understood, in a strange way. She'd felt very protective of her own little house when Nessa tore into the homes in this area, calling them trash. "I'm sorry. I'm just a tad on edge right now."

He was staring at the fox, who was now trying to wrap himself around his leg, like a cat. He shook it off a little. "I thought you got rid of this thing."

"No. I have to. I mean, I will. Soon." She bit her tongue at the very thought.

"So why'd you come back? You get lost?"

Audrey tilted her head at him. "No. I basically got stopped at the border by the police and told to turn around."

"Seriously?" His mouth hung open. "They're throwing up roadblocks for little ol' you?"

"I guess."

"So you didn't get to talk to the wife."

"Supposedly, they already did. And she's clear. Anyway, I can't leave here until someone figures out whoever killed the foreman," she said, patting her thigh. "Come on, Nick. Let's go to prison, I mean, home."

She cringed as the word left her mouth. Home. *Well, it's my home, but it won't be home for you, Nick, much longer.* Oblivious, he scampered into her arms like a well-trained house pet and licked the side of her face.

Mason eyed the thing with disgust. "Like I told you, girl. Just let the police handle the thing. They got a hold on it. I'm sure."

She cast him a doubtful look.

"Look, don't go accusing them of not being able to find their backsides with both hands. They got this. Sounds like they're doing everything right. What more do you want from them?"

She scowled at him. But maybe he was right. After all, they were right on her tail when she tried to leave town. They'd already investigated Fabri's wife. Maybe she just needed to concentrate on her renovations and forget about it.

If only it were that easy.

She walked home silently, thinking, with Nick following faithfully at her heels. It was hard to think of anything else with everyone looking at her like she was guilty. It almost made her *feel* guilty. And every time Nick made a sound behind her, she only felt guiltier.

When she got home, she noticed the windows were wide open in Nessa's house, the curtains blowing in the breeze. Classical music

133

wafted out. Audrey peered inside. Despite the order to cease renovations, Nessa was going full-bore with her internal décor—an entire wall inside had been painted in a peach and white checkerboard pattern, and there was shiplap everywhere. So chic.

Audrey was glad that despite the open windows, Nessa was nowhere in sight.

She quickly and silently slipped inside her own house and looked around. After seeing all the beauty across the street, and the bad day she'd had, her own place only seemed worse than she remembered.

Yes, take a page from Nessa's playbook. Press on with the renovations.

The first thing she did when she got inside was grab another apple, since she was starving. She finished it while Nick attacked the kibble in the soup bowl she'd left near his little nest in the corner of the kitchen. As he did, she wondered if there was a way around Officer Ricci's "no wild animals" edict. After all, Nick pretty much came and went as he pleased. This wasn't much different from leaving food outside for a stray, was it?

Besides, as she looked at his little paw, she could see the scar from the fence. The bandage was long gone, but the wound was still there. He was still injured.

She couldn't just throw him out. That wouldn't be fair. It wouldn't be *humane*.

Forget about that now. Concentrate on the renovations.

Tossing the apple core in the trash, she crouched in front of the latest delivery she'd gotten from the hardware store—a railing for the staircase. Yes, the staircase was narrow, but it was also very steep, so while a small railing would impinge on the precious little real estate in the hallway, it would also probably save a few necks from breaking. A definite plus.

She grabbed her cordless drill from the toolbox and made quick work of fastening the brackets to the wall that would hold the slim iron railing up. Then she drilled in the screws to attach the iron to the brackets. This was the stuff she was great at. Her father used to call her the Drillmaster.

She smiled as she finished a half hour later, realizing that yes, making herself busy *had* actually helped. She hadn't thought about the murder, hardly at all.

She placed her drill back into the toolbox as Nick wandered into the stairwell to see what she was up to. "See?" she said to him. "Small changes, little by little … we'll make this house a home in no time."

Stooping over, she jiggled the railing to make sure it was steady.

And it—and half of the plaster on the wall—came off in her hands.

Partly because it was so heavy, and partly because she hadn't expected it, the thing hit the stairs with a terrific crash and slid the rest of the way down the stairwell, filling the narrow space with such a massive amount of dust that Audrey couldn't see a thing. All she heard was Nick, letting out a snarl as he dove out of the way of the sliding railing.

When the dust cleared, not only did she not have a railing, but there were also three massive holes in the wall.

She wanted to cry.

Instead, she laughed.

She laughed so long, and so hard, that she sounded insane, even to herself.

She hadn't checked her bank account in days, but she knew for sure it was under a thousand dollars. This new repair would only siphon more money away. When she'd moved here, she'd hoped she would've been able to get her license by now and start vet work. Now, that seemed like an eternity away.

For the first time in a while, she thought of the Brit she'd run into at La Mela Verde. He'd been at the end of his rope, too. Maybe he'd packed it in. Maybe he was already back in London, where things made sense.

She hadn't thought about giving up in days. But now, the overreaching feeling came and planted itself, hard, in her head: Maybe she should be back in Boston, too.

Wiping plaster dust from her face and hair, she left the railing where it'd come to rest and climbed the stairs to her bedroom. Throwing herself on the unmade bed, she grabbed her phone and stared at the display, wanting desperately to have a lifeline to back home.

And miraculously, there it was.

She'd have preferred Brina, but she did get *someone* in Boston. There were three calls from Back Bay Animal Care, and one voicemail.

She frowned. What did they want? Probably to figure out whether she planned on continuing her benefits or something. She pressed the voicemail link and held the phone to her ear.

"Hi, there, Dr. Smart. It's Dr. Carey. I hope you're doing well," the voicemail said, and was it her imagination or did her former supervisor sound ridiculously apologetic? "I've been in discussions with the Board of Directors about finding your replacement and we've come to the conclusion that we'd be remiss in not contacting you and giving you the option to return."

Audrey sat up straight, clutching the phone hard to her ear.

"Our hopes are that you made the decision rather quickly and that perhaps upon further thought you may have changed your mind. If so, well, why don't you give me a call to discuss this? I'll be in the office all day. Hope everything is well with you."

Now, that was interesting.

She could have her old job back. It wasn't gone for good. All she needed to do was step on a plane heading west. She could be back in Boston, a veterinarian, treating real patients, in no time.

A little thrill went through her at the thought.

Then she remembered the little stand-off she'd had with Officer Ricci at the Mussomeli city limits.

Still, the second she was cleared to leave … she could, and a job would be waiting for her.

Settling down among her pillows, Audrey returned the call. She got one of the receptionists. "Hi, Mindy. It's Audrey Smart. I'm returning Dr. Carey's call."

"Oh, Dr. Smart! Yes, Dr. Carey was anxious to speak with you. I'll patch you right in."

Barely a second later, the phone clicked and Dr. Carey's no-nonsense voice came through, this time tinged with concern. "Audrey?"

"Yes, hi, Dr. Carey. How are you?"

"I'm fine. We're all fine here. Well, we're a little short-staffed, but we have our health."

"Short-staffed?"

"Oh. You didn't hear? Unfortunately Dr. Watts announced his departure. He and one of the techs ran off together, apparently, without any prior notice."

Audrey's eyes bulged. "And … Dr. Ferris?"

"He's fine. Obviously a little overworked, since we haven't been able to replace your position yet."

Serves him right, she thought bitterly. "I'm sorry to hear that. I wish I could help you, but I'm sure you haven't heard, I'm in—"

"Sicily. We know."

She blinked. "You do?"

"I wanted to do this in person, so I visited your apartment. Your landlord informed me that you'd gone overseas." She laughed a little, a sound that Audrey wasn't quite used to hearing. "But that's what airplanes are for, right? And rather than going through a drawn-out

136

process of trying to hire another doctor whose work we're not familiar with, we thought it made sense to do our due diligence and see if you would be amenable to perhaps returning, if your situation and perspective had changed at all."

"Oh. Wow." That wasn't the smooth, diplomatic response she'd wanted to give, but she couldn't help it. Her mouth was hanging open. "I want you to know, I didn't make the decision on the spur of the moment. It was a long time coming, something that had been brewing to a head over many months of—"

"I understand. I wish you'd have voiced your dissatisfaction to me sooner. I could've nipped whatever problems you were having in the bud."

"One of the problems is still there. Dr. Ferris. He's ..." *A big, total jerkface.* "Not exactly easy to get along with."

"Oh, you don't think I know that?" Now, she really laughed, which was crazy. Dr. Carey was talking to Audrey like a friend, not a supervisor. It felt like a bond was being forged, even across all those miles separating them. "I have to field complaints almost weekly from techs who claim they'd been treated as second-class citizens by him. He's a prima donna. And Dr. Watts was a sexual harassment lawsuit waiting to happen. In fact, *you* were the only doctor I could rely on who didn't have that excess baggage. You were solid, Audrey. Very solid."

"Really?" She'd never been this comfortable with Dr. Carey. In fact, she might have even used her first name, if she'd known it. "Um, well, thanks."

"So that's why—and I'm sorry it's taken a while but I've just cleared it with the board—the clinic is prepared to offer you a raise of twenty thousand dollars a year."

Audrey's eyes bulged. Was she talking to the right Dr. Smart?

"Oh," was all she could get out, for the longest time. "That's generous."

"Yes, I thought you'd be pleased. And we will be replacing Dr. Watts with a small animal specialist so we wouldn't expect you to take on any extra shifts."

She nodded. It sounded so good. That extra money in her paycheck would mean the difference between that cruddy apartment in Southie and a nice place, right there in the Back Bay. Plus, she and Dr. Carey had mutual respect, solidarity, an understanding, now. And she'd be back home, where things made sense.

If only she didn't have to worry about Officer Ricci following her to the airport. How would she ever get away?

"Um … I wonder if I could have a few days to think it over?" she asked. *Or a few days to see if I'm finally cleared to leave town?*

"Oh, of course. But please, I can't give you more than forty-eight hours. I meet with the board in two days and I have to give them your decision. All right?"

That was cutting it close. But she didn't have a choice. "Yes. Thank you."

"All right, thanks, Audrey. Have a good day."

Dr. Carey ended the call, leaving Audrey lying in her bed, looking up at the water-stained ceiling, completely immobile.

Maybe this was a sign?

When she finally picked her jaw up off the floor, she called Brina.

Brina answered and snapped, "Well, it's about time."

True, back in Boston, Audrey was in the habit of calling her sister almost every day. But it hadn't been an eternity since they last spoke, just a few days. But so much had happened in those days. "Do you think you could send me some money?"

"Really? You drop off the face of the earth and then you tell me you need money?"

"Brina. Everything has been way more expensive than I expected. I only have a thousand dollars left in my account. I thought I'd be able to get my license by now and start doing house calls, but I've run into a few roadblocks."

"Fine. I'll send you a thousand bucks. Now, no apologies for disappearing? I thought I'd see your face on a milk carton."

"Sorry. I've been busy."

"Doing what?"

"Oh, getting accused of a murder, trying to clear my name. Fun stuff like that."

A pause. "Very funny."

"I'm not joking. A guy across the street fell off a cliff. I found the body. So I'm a suspect."

"Oh my god! Are you serious? That's terrible." A pause. "Wait … is this the guy from the construction site that was making all that noise the other day?"

Audrey sighed. "Yes. He and I got into a little squabble the day before. I went over to apologize to him, and I found him." She winced, trying to fight back the memory of his mangled body on the ground below her.

"Oh, no! Sweetie, that must've been awful! Why didn't you call me?"

"Like I said. I've been busy."

"They're not going to arrest you, are they? If they do, I'll sic Max on them. You tell them that," she said, indignant.

"He's an IP attorney."

"So?" That was Brina's problem. She really thought her husband could do no wrong. "He is part of the biggest firm in the city. He knows people. You'll have the best legal defense they've ever seen in that one-horse town."

"Okay, hold on. Let's not get carried away. They haven't arrested me. They're still investigating," she said, eyes volleying around the bedroom. Everywhere she looked, she saw something that needed TLC. At a nice Back Bay Apartment, she could probably have multiple bedrooms. A view of the skyline. A doorman. A non-possessed shower. "I wanted to call you because I just got off the phone with Dr. Carey, from Back Bay Animal Care."

"Let me guess. They want you back."

Audrey paused, dumbstruck. "Wait. How did you know that?"

"Because you're awesome. Duh. Continue."

Once again, Brina was the all-knowing Buddha. "She's offering me a substantial raise. And even better, Dr. Watts actually left. She told me that I was the best doctor there, because I didn't have all the drama. Can you believe that?"

"Of course I can. Because it's true," she said, matter-of-factly. "So, are you going to take it?"

She bit her lip. "I don't know. That's why I called you. What do you think?"

"Don't be a goofball. Of course I think you should. But for purely selfish reasons. I miss your face."

Audrey smiled. "I miss you, too."

"And also, I think it might be a good idea to skip town before they lock you in prison. I saw a Lifetime movie on that, once. Girl got locked in some prison in a third world country and she didn't speak the language, and I think all she had was a speeding ticket," Brina said in a conspiratorial whisper. "For a murder, you'd probably get the firing squad."

Audrey winced. "Well, that makes me feel better."

"So, fly away home! Let me know when your flight gets in and I'll meet you at Logan."

"It's not that easy."

"Sure it is. I'm on Expedia right now. There's a flight that leaves from Palermo in three hours."

139

Audrey sighed. "Actually. The police told me that I can't leave town."

"What? Not at all?"

"Not at all."

"Is that even legal? You're an American! I'll ask Max about—"

"No. It's fine. Besides, I'm not sure I want to take the job yet. I need to think on it more."

Brina blew out a big breath of air. "Really? Why? You have no money left. You said the house is a wreck. Now you're accused of a murder. You really think it could get any worse? I mean, why would you even bother staying? You can have everything you had before, but better!"

She swallowed. *Everything you had before.*

Meaning bitter cold Boston winters. Lonely nights eating leftover Thai in an empty apartment. Years upon years of high school reunions with absolutely nothing of significance to brag about.

"Hello? You still there?" Brina said, knocking her out of her desolate thoughts.

"I am. I'm just thinking, how much better? Because it wasn't just the crappy Southie apartment and Dr. Watts that bothered me. It was everything. The monotony of life. The knowledge that this was what I had to look forward to for the next fifty years. I don't know if hopping on a plane back to that life is the answer. This may be insane, it may be an uphill battle, but it's different, at least."

"*Very* different. You may have the inside of a prison cell to look forward to if you stay. Or worse, the firing squad!"

Audrey groaned. "They don't do that anymore."

"Are you sure?"

"I'll let you know what I decide," she said, ending the call.

She slipped out of the bed and went to the window. Maybe this would be the last view of freedom she'd ever have.

CHAPTER TWENTY SEVEN

Audrey woke the following morning to a loud banging on the front door.

She sat up, a bolt of fear ripping through her. It was the kind of knocking the police did, right before they rammed down the door and arrested whoever was inside.

Grabbing her robe, she threw it over her tank top and shorts and was just tying the tie when she noticed the cop car outside.

Oh, no.

Her hand trembled as she reached for the door. When she opened it, she almost expected to be cuffed and led outside.

Instead, Officer Ricci hung on the door frame, looking tired, lips twisted to one side. "I've been knocking for ten minutes."

"Oh." She let out a relieved sigh. "Sorry. I didn't realize. I didn't sleep very well last night, and I guess I was catching up."

She'd spent the evening mulling over her options. Honestly, as Mason was so kind to point out, she really didn't have many. Unless she planned to Von Trapp it over the mountains in the dead of night and escape to the airport, she had to stay put.

But as she slept, her mind kept reeling back to that overwhelming sense of suffocation she'd felt living in Boston. She could have a new place, a better working situation, but would it matter? Everything else would be the same. *She'd* still be the same. And she'd have left Sicily without completing her mission. Her mission to fix up a house and live in it and experience all of what living abroad had to offer. Her father would be so disappointed.

Ricci's eyes trailed down to the ground and his frown deepened. "Yesterday was a warning. You were let off easy. It won't be repeated."

She nodded. "I understand, and I appreciate ..."

She stopped when she realized what he was staring at. Nick was sitting right beside her, licking his paws, enjoying the entertainment.

Oh, she mouthed, red-faced. "I know. I have to get rid of him. And I will. It's not that easy, though."

Ricci scowled. "*Si,* it *is* that easy. You take him to the side of the road, say your goodbyes, and drive away. The end. Easy."

"No. You see, he's injured. And he's a good tracker. If I dropped him anywhere in town, he'd likely just find his way back." She shrugged innocently. "He follows me around. I tried to lock him out. He's been getting in and out of the house—somehow—I don't even know how!"

The officer hooked a finger at her, motioning her outside. As much as she didn't want to go out in just a robe, her hair looking like a bird's nest, she knew she was skating on thin ice. She padded out onto the street, the cobblestones cold under her feet, and followed him to the side of the house. He pointed to the crumbling corner of the home, where, if she stooped, she could see a damp, moldy area, and beyond that, light. Actually, the tiles of her bathroom. And … was that her shower?

Mystery solved. And yet, it presented another mystery. How many townspeople had used that hole to peep in on her when she was bathing?

Sickness swirled in her stomach. "Lovely."

"I'd close that up quickly, if I were you."

She nodded. "I will. But even if I do block the hole up, he'll find another way in. He's clever." She laced her fingers together, begging him for more time. "I'd need to go outside the city limits, *far* outside the city limits, and I can't … right?"

Ricci crossed his arms. "I don't care. Either you do it, or I'll have animal control handle it. And I promise you that they will not be as nice to the animal."

She sighed. "I guess …"

"Trust me. Do it today. And that should solve your unwanted houseguest situation."

Actually, as far as unwanted houseguests went, Officer Ricci ranked higher than the fox. But Audrey wasn't about to tell him that. "I appreciate it," she told him, her voice mechanical. "I'll take care of it—and him—right away."

As she said the words, the little fox nudged her leg, pointed ears turned in her direction. Was it her, or did he understand everything that was being said?

Her face fell. She clutched her stomach. The idea of getting rid of him, leaving him to the wild? It made her feel physically ill.

"Come now, Audrey. You are a doctor of animal care. You know an animal like that belongs in the wild. Not in a home."

She certainly did know that. But the knowledge didn't make her feel any better.

Audrey didn't want to borrow Mason's car again, considering he was such a massive diva.

So later that day, after spoiling Nick, giving him cuddles and filling him up with plenty of fruity treats—more apples and a little bit of honeydew—she put him in a basket and set out walking with him, downhill.

The uphill walk would be her punishment for abandoning this poor creature.

But she wasn't, she kept reminding herself. He was wild. Free. The world was his home. He didn't belong to her. And he was better off out in nature, with his other fox friends.

She meandered aimlessly up and down the streets, hoping that wherever she went, he'd be confused by the scent. She wasn't exactly sure where she planned to leave him, but she wanted someplace perfect. Green. Shady. With plenty of area to scamper about. So that took her far out of the city proper.

She'd probably walked five miles by the time she came to someplace suitable. It was a grassy field, with a dilapidated old shed in the distance, close to caving in. Sweat beaded on her brow as she stopped to rest at a rock on the side of the road.

Audrey looked around and took a deep breath. She'd have to do it now, before she lost her nerve.

Opening the side of the basket, she mentally prepared herself for his adorable little furry face. When he peeked up at her, she realized all the preparation in the world wouldn't be enough. He crawled into the corner of the basket and wrapped his tail around himself, and shook his head slightly. It was almost as if he was begging, *Please don't do this.*

She felt the seams of her composure ripping, ripping, ripping … and then suddenly, tears began to fall. A second later, she was weeping on the side of the road, so hard, a car stopped. The driver, an old man, called something to her in Italian, but she was sobbing too hard to speak. She simply waved him on.

"Come on, now, Nick. I want you to go on. Have a good life. Make lots of nice fox friends …" she blubbered, sniffling. "It isn't so bad. You'll have lots of fun out there, much more fun than you've been having with me. I promise!"

But her voice was so weak, even she didn't believe it.

She had to do it quick, like ripping off a Band-Aid.

Only thing was, he wouldn't get out of the basket. She tipped it to the side, but he stayed propped in his corner. She scooped him out, but he took a swipe at her. Finally, she tipped it over entirely, and he rolled gently out, onto the ground, like a red carpet.

The first thing he did was scamper back to the basket, but she lifted it up before he could take refuge in it. She shooed him. "Go on. Out onto the fields. Run. Scamper. Cavort. You'll have plenty of fun adventures."

He stared at her, then tilted his head.

"I'm not going to say it again!" She stamped her foot, angrier at herself for getting attached than at him. "Go on!"

After a moment's hesitation, he ran toward her, wrapped his tail around her calf like a mink stole, let out a little purr of appreciation, then turned and darted off into the field, chasing after a moth. When he got about halfway to the shack, he paused and turned to look at her.

Before she could wave, he hung a right and went directly to a chain-link fence. He walked the perimeter of it for a little while, and then slipped into a hole beneath it.

An overwhelming sense of dread fell over her then. Sure, she'd been alone all this time, but she'd never felt so alone as at that moment.

She walked toward the fence, wondering what kind of business it belonged to. Just beyond the fence, there was a large shed with a corrugated roof. It was only when she walked around to the front of the enclosure that she saw the piles and piles of lumber stacked neatly inside. On the fence, a large sign proclaimed: *Altera Ditta di Legnami.*

She couldn't read it, but she could guess what it said. The "A" in Altera was made to look like a few pieces of lumber, nailed together. Cute.

But a distinct feeling of déjà vu crept over her.

She'd seen that logo before.

Her mind spiraled back to that day, when she'd been standing at the front stoop, watching the junk from the renovation project falling at her feet. There'd been all kinds of things—old pipes, nails, trash, tools … but also, a bunch of pieces of lumber with the *Altera* logo stamped upon them, in red.

Something struck her then.

Fabri had been looking at that lumber, saying something that she couldn't understand. And he'd been looking up at his cousin, but was it possible that he wasn't talking to the cousin at all? Maybe he'd been muttering under his breath about the lumber supplier.

Maybe …

She blinked out of her thoughts to see Nick standing on the other side of the fence, looking at her, like, *What are you going to do?*

"Right," she said to him, making the decision. She reached into her pocket, pulled out her phone, and dialed the general number for the police. When a receptionist answered, she said, "*Ciao.* Detective DiNardo, *per favore.*"

The receptionist said a bunch of words, only two of which Audrey understood. *Mi dispiace.* I'm sorry.

She tried again. "Officer Ricci, then?"

This time, the call was put through. A moment later, a deep male voice said, "*Si?*"

"Officer Ricci? It's me, Audrey Smart."

"Ah. Audrey. Calling me to tell me that you've had success in getting rid of your problem, yes?"

She stared at her "problem" through the fence. "Actually, no. Not exactly." She could almost sense the frustration coming through the phone lines. "I mean, I was going to, I was headed to the outskirts of town to bring him somewhere where he would be happy, and not be able to find his way back, but then I got to this place, and I saw this logo, and I had an idea and it all cemented in my head, like boom—"

"Wait. Slow down. What is this all about?"

She took a deep breath. Fanned her face. The sun was beating down on her, making her feel dizzy, like she might faint. She clutched the phone tighter to her ear and looked around to make sure no one was nearby. Her voice, when it came out, was barely a breath, and so tense that it crackled.

"I think I might know who killed Ernesto Fabri."

CHAPTER TWENTY EIGHT

There was dead air on the other end of the phone for so long, Audrey thought that she'd lost the connection. "Hello?"

"I'm here," Officer Ricci said at last, and in those two words, she could tell one undeniable fact: He thought she was off her rocker.

"I'm serious. I feel like you should be casing this joint, or whatever you guys do."

"Casing ... ?" he began, confused. "Let's back up. Where, exactly, are you?"

"Altera Lumber," she said, peering through the links of the fence. Sure enough, there were a few men walking about in hard hats and jeans, and farther inside, a large red outbuilding, along with a smaller trailer with a sign that said, *Ufficio*. "So are you going to call me backup?"

"Backup? Wait. Audrey. Let's take a deep breath, okay?"

"No, I'm going to talk to them, at least. That's all. If I have to do it alone, then fine."

There was a pause. "Wait. Audrey. Detective DiNardo just walked in." He started to say something in Italian, probably, *Maybe you can talk some sense into this lunatic,* and then there was a brief shuffling on the other end.

Finally, a voice said, "Dottore Smart?"

"Yes. Detective DiNardo?" She let out a sigh of relief. At least Ricci had ushered her up the chain of command instead of hanging up on her. "I'm here on the outskirts of town and I think I've discovered someone, or a group of people, who might be responsible for Fabri's death."

"And how did you do that?" He seemed slightly annoyed.

"Honestly, I wasn't poking my nose where it didn't belong. Believe me. Totally by chance, while I was walking out here, I stumbled upon a lumber company, Altera, and I remembered hearing that Fabri was getting into all sorts of trouble for bad deals. And this Altera, I remember, supplied the lumber for the—"

"Altera?"

"Yes! You know it?"

"Of course I do. I know Signore Altera. Very well, in fact."

Oh, no. Here it comes. He's his cousin. "Well, I think someone should question him because he definitely provided the lumber, and I think that if he screwed him out of money, that's a good motive as any—"

"Stop. You're right. But *we'll* question him. *Not* you. Do you understand?"

"Oh. Yes. Of course."

"Go home, Dottore Smart. Please. That's an order."

She knew that was coming. She sighed. "All right. Fine. I will. But … could you let me know what happens?"

"Audrey," he said simply. Then he hung up.

So, that was a no?

She pocketed her phone and looked at Nick through the fence. She crouched in front of him. "I know, right?" she said, sticking her fingers through a link to pet the top of his head. "What a rip-off. I provide a possible case-cracking tip and they won't even let me know the outcome."

He bowed his head into her pets, clearly on her side.

"All right, goofball," she said to him, standing. "You are a crazy little fox. If you want to stay here among the lumber, fine. I'm no fox. But I think you'd be happier in the green wilderness."

She turned to leave, and this time, he whimpered.

"I'm sorry. You heard the detective. I've got to split."

She took all of two steps before he whimpered even louder.

"Oh, come on, little one. Don't carry on so much. You're going to get me in trouble. And you're going to be fine."

This time, when she turned away, she meant to keep heading along the road, without stopping until she got back to her house.

But just then, behind her, a man's voice called out urgently in Italian. "*Vattene! Vattene, bastardo!*"

She whirled to find a man rushing toward her with an old wicker broom. He was older, and his white T-shirt barely covered his pot belly, similar to Ernesto. He was wearing suspenders and dress shoes, and was hairless on top with impressive sideburns on his cheeks. His face was ruddy and twisted in anger.

Just like she knew what *assassina* meant, so was she sure about *bastardo*. He started to swing the broom haphazardly in all directions, too much exertion to expend on such a tiny and cute little mongrel who was doing absolutely nothing wrong. Almost embarrassed for him, Nick easily avoided the swipes, jumped to the top of a lumber pile, and looked down at the man, like, *Silly human.*

147

"What are you doing?" Audrey shouted. She already didn't like him, because hello? A furry creature does not deserve to be battered with a broom, even though from the way the man was now rasping for breath, he was the one who'd clearly gotten the worst of it. "It's just a poor, defenseless animal."

He narrowed his eyes at her. "American?" He said it as if the word was synonymous with "idiot." "Those stupid mongrels come in here and poop all over the supplies. I can't keep them out. I need to electrify this fence, that's what I need to do."

He was entirely serious. She gasped. "Are you freaking kidding me?"

He shrugged. "What do you care about it? That your pet?"

"No," she said immediately, because she didn't need to be in any more trouble than she already was. "But it doesn't matter. They're living creatures. They should be treated with respect."

"They're on my property," he growled, shaking his fist up at the fox. *Bastardo.*"

"*Your* property?" She blinked. She knew what she'd told the detective, but this man had held her up. Besides, she couldn't simply walk away. She could ask a few innocent questions, then let the police take over when they arrived. "So this is your place?"

He nodded. "That's my name on the sign. Bernardo Altera."

Her instincts prickled. It might have been the way he treated Nick, but something about this made her finally feel like she was on the right path.

"Oh. I've heard about you," she said, then wondered if she shouldn't have said that when he looked surprised. "I mean, I've seen your stamp on lumber. I'm working on a project, renovating a house myself. I could use some of your supplies."

His demeanor changed in the blink of an eye. He smiled. "Is that so? Well, come in my office. I provide you a quote."

Audrey checked over her shoulder, expecting to see DiNardo and Ricci barreling toward her, sirens flashing and guns drawn. But the street out of town was empty. She looked up at Nick, who'd made himself comfortable at the top of the pile.

"All right, fine," she said. After all, it was broad daylight. There were construction workers around. Not exactly the stuff of a murder mystery show. She'd be fine.

She shifted her empty basket to the other arm and followed him beyond the gates, into the yard. As they walked toward the trailer,

Altera pointed out a load of lumber. "That? That is good. Good price on it. You like."

She wasn't sure if that was a question, but she nodded anyway. As far as she was concerned, lumber was lumber. Her dad might've had more of an opinion, but to her, it all looked the same.

Really, all she wanted to find out was one thing, and it wasn't the price of the supplies. She wanted to know where he was the morning that Ernesto Fabri had been killed.

And it wouldn't hurt to ask a few more questions.

After all, the police would be there soon. Better to beg forgiveness than ask permission.

"You buy one of these cheap properties, yes?" he asked her as he held the door open for her. "The one euro?"

She walked inside, turning to see if the police were arriving yet. No, the street was empty, as far as the eye could see. Nick was busy hopping from plank to plank, trying to get down from the heap. She almost didn't hear the question. "Um, yes, I did. Piazza Tre."

The trailer was remarkably tiny inside and almost painfully messy with open file cabinets teeming with papers. Papers on every surface, too. A fan in the corner hummed away, oscillating slowly, making the papers ruffle slightly, but the rush of air did nothing to dispel the strong stench of garlic.

There wasn't much of a walkway between the furniture. Altera squeezed between a file cabinet and the side of a desk and stood in front of a plastic chair that made an unflattering noise as he lowered his substantial body into it. Meanwhile, Audrey watched him carefully, waiting for some sign of recognition. But he didn't appear to make the connection to the murder that had happened there. He simply grabbed a pad and pen and scribbled it down. "Now, what work are you having done?"

Maybe she was wrong. "Um … well …" She hadn't really thought about it. She took the folding chair across from him and noticed a wall calendar there, scribbled with various job names. She scanned to the date of the murder, squinting to read the terrible handwriting.

He noticed her looking, so she quickly averted her eyes.

"All of it. I mean, I guess I um, should just start with the subfloor?"

He wrote something down and went to grab his calculator. As he did, she leaned forward and read what was written on the calendar. Not *Fabri*. It said, *Cappeli, 10.*

He turned back to her just as she was straightening up. "All right. How big?"

"Not very. I guess … what's the smallest amount I can get?"

He rambled on about prices, telling her she could have just about any amount of lumber, but a delivery fee would apply to quantities under two hundred euros. She wasn't really listening. She was thinking about the calendar. Because if he was due at the Cappeli project at ten, that gave him plenty of time to be at Nessa's beforehand. She wracked her brain, trying to think of a way to swerve the conversation to what she really wanted to know.

Finally, while he was in mid-sentence, she blurted, "My friend across the street. She used your lumber."

He looked up from his pad, obviously expecting more.

What were you expecting, Audrey? For him to say, "Oh, is that at the place where I offed the foreman?"

"She said this place was the best in town," she continued, really talking out of her backside now.

But Altera seemed to buy it. He smiled. "Good to hear. I agree."

"Of course, she wasn't doing the renovations herself," she continued, her eyes ping-ponging around the room. There was a stack of metal filing cabinets on one side. The top one actually had a little index card on the front that said, *A-Fabri.* "She used a construction company. Fabri Fratelli?"

His eyes blinked to hers, and for a split second, she saw recognition there. But he didn't say anything. He pulled out what looked like a triple-layer quote form and started to fill it out.

"You probably knew them well?" she goaded.

He shook his head. "We work with thousands of customers. I don't know them all. Name?"

For a moment, she wondered if she should leave an alias. But that would have her look even more suspicious. Besides, if he proved to be innocent, she'd need to get her lumber from *somewhere*. "Audrey Smart. I'm surprised. They're pretty big. So you didn't hear about the foreman? Ernesto Fabri?"

He shook his head again, still writing information. "Phone number?"

She gave it to him. "It's odd you never met him. He seemed to be in business a while. He actually died on the site. It was a fall. Some say he was murdered."

He looked up suddenly, eyes narrowed, and dropped the pen to the paper. "What's this all about? Who are you?"

"Just …" She waved her hand vaguely. Maybe this was a mistake. Her voice came out as a squeak. "Buying lumber, is all."

His eyes narrowed. "I don't believe that. What are you really here for?"

She stood up so abruptly the basket fell from her lap. She stooped to pick it up. "Nothing. I was just making small talk, but if you're not interested, I guess I'll take my business elsewhere."

Audrey lifted her chin, indignant, and whirled to reach for the door.

The second she did, though, Bernardo Altera, who was much sprier than she gave him credit for, came around the desk and lodged his body in between her and her escape. He crossed his arms. "I don't think so."

She swallowed as she looked out the window. Nope. No police cars yet. She was alone.

You've miscalculated, Audrey.

He took a step toward her, forcing her back until she could feel the hard edge of his metal desk against the backs of her thighs. This close, his breath was rancid. "Start talking. Tell me what you know."

CHAPTER TWENTY NINE

Audrey still hadn't found her voice. The man might have been older, but his neck was as thick as a tree trunk and his arms bulged at his sides. It wouldn't take very much to pummel her into the floorboards. Right here. In broad daylight. Even with construction workers milling about outside, the sound of the forklift whirring outside could easily drown out her screams.

"Look. I don't want any trouble," she said, reaching for the door handle again.

This time, he put a hand on her shoulder and shoved her back. A small movement, and yet pain tore down her arm. "Then you shouldn't have come looking for it."

Oh, God. He really could kill me.

"The police are going to be here any minute," she said, voice trembling. At least, she hoped.

That had the opposite effect of what she wanted. His face flooded with red and he gnashed his teeth. "You call the police? For what? You're bluffing."

"I'm not." She managed to skirt around the desk, into the aisle, and started backing up more, with him advancing two steps for every one she took. "But you have a reason to be worried, right? It was you, wasn't it? You were in on it with him, helping him bump up the costs. Did he give you a cut, was that it?"

Altera's eyes burned into hers. He punched his open hand, like he wanted to do the same to her head. His voice was low. "You know nothing."

But in that moment, she knew that she was on the right track. He had no reason to behave this suspiciously unless he had something to hide. "So what happened? Did you argue? Did one of you decide to get a little too greedy? Did you try to strike a deal, and he said he'd go to another supplier if you didn't accept his terms?"

He froze. His lips puckered.

I've got him, she thought, exhilarated. "And so, what? You gave him an ultimatum. You went to Piazza Due early in the morning, and he gave you an answer you didn't like. Things got heated, and you shoved him over the side of the cliff. Right?"

"It was an accident," he said, his voice so low she could barely hear it.

Holy ... she thought, her body breaking out in goose bumps. *I'm right? I'm actually right?*

He stared at her, aghast. "How did you know?"

"Honestly ... I didn't know, until just this minute. I had a hunch. That's all."

His eyes narrowed. "Then the police aren't coming ..." He started to advance on her again.

She took a step back. "No! They are!" she cried, but she was too late. His hands shot out, ready to grab for her neck. Before he could wrap them around her throat, she ducked out of the way and slipped around him, grabbing the small fan and holding it between them as she squeezed into a corner. The trailer was already suffocatingly small, but now she was really trapped.

She let out a yelp and held the fan up. "Don't, or I'll ..."

The moment he lunged for her, though, a furry blur appeared in the periphery of her vision, scampering under the windows. It jumped, hanging in mid-air for a split second before connecting with Altera's thick body, sending him stumbling back.

She looked down just long enough to see Nick bury his teeth in the man's hairy forearm, right above his gold watch.

He wailed in pain. She dove for escape, climbing over the desk and scuttling for the door. She went to hold it open for Nick, but he'd already gotten through ahead of her.

"Clever fox," she said as she escaped into the air, about to make a run for it.

But she didn't have to. A police car pulled up in a cloud of dust, making her choke. It was slightly less dramatic than she'd expected after the call she'd made to them. Actually, a lot less dramatic. No flashing lights or sirens, and they didn't have their guns drawn. No backup. Just the two of them.

Before they could even get out of the car, she started to unload on them.

"Guys," she said breathlessly, pointing at the trailer. "Bernardo Altera. He's your man. He confessed to me. He was in business with—"

She stopped when she realized he was standing behind her, holding his bloody wrist. Scowling at her.

She moved safely behind Officer Ricci's body. "Ask him," she said in a small voice. "Go on."

153

They all looked at Altera expectantly. She thought for sure he'd deny it, but he simply said, "It was an accident. But he was a scum. I'm sure a lot of people are better off in this world without him in it. He scammed hundreds of people. I just wanted him to stop."

"Bull! You were in on it with him!" Audrey shouted, but Detective DiNardo held up his hand.

"You can tell us all about it down at the station," DiNardo said, motioning to Ricci, who removed his cuffs from his belt and snapped them behind Altera's back.

As Ricci led Altera back to the police car, Audrey did her best to avoid the newly apprehended man's death stare. Meanwhile, DiNardo looked at her. "So much for going home, eh?"

She smiled innocently. "I got held up."

He let out a laugh and looked at the ground, where Nick was busy sniffing at his shoes. "And so much for getting rid of him."

She hitched a shoulder. "I can't help it. He follows me everywhere."

"I suppose this time, that's a good thing. Looks like he helped you out of a bad situation."

"Yes." She smiled down at him. Then she looked up at DiNardo, hopeful. "Does that mean I can …"

"No. Not at all," he said, and turned to go back to the car.

So that's the gratitude I get for cracking the case, she thought, sighing as Nick planted himself between her feet, her little guard dog.

But actually, that was all right. She was all right. She was free. Free to go anywhere in the world now.

And yet the only place she really wanted to go was right back to Piazza Tre.

Home.

CHAPTER THIRTY

Audrey never realized how good she had it. Her little house was great. As she rolled over in bed in the morning sunlight and smiled up at the water-stained ceiling, thinking just how artistic the shapes were, she realized that life was really great.

She looked over at Nick, who was still lounging on her bed, between the pillows, and smiled.

She would never let Nick go. Even if it put her in jail.

Downstairs, she could hear Mason hammering on her wall, helping her as he'd promised. Bit by bit, the place was coming together.

Everything was great.

Last night, she'd made a list of everything she needed to do. And she couldn't help smiling, thinking of all of it. Even the drudge jobs. It would be fun, because it was everything her father would've loved. She was definitely her father's daughter.

She picked up her phone and called Back Bay Animal Care. Though it was the middle of the night in Boston, it rang through to the emergency line, and Dr. Carey, who must've been on call that night, picked up.

"Oh, Audrey!" she said, and Audrey could hear the hopefulness in her voice. "I was hoping you'd call."

Audrey said, "Dr. Carey, I'm sorry, but it's not good news." *For you, anyway.* "As much as I appreciate your offer, I just moved to Sicily and I'm finding my way around here. I don't want to give it up quite yet."

"Oh." The disappointment was obvious, but Dr. Carey was, as always, tactful and diplomatic. "That's too bad. I'm sure everyone will be sorry to hear it. I know I am."

She hung up and took a deep breath. That was it. She had burned all her bridges. Now she had no choice but to make her new life in Sicily work.

Audrey took a deep breath. She needed a miracle, probably, if she was ever going to get her vet practice started. There were applications to fill out, board review, months and months of waiting … and meanwhile, her bank account was suffering. Luckily, she'd learned she could take a cash advance from her credit card, and she planned to do that to pay for supplies at the hardware store. But she needed to do something, soon, in order to maintain a livelihood.

At least she wasn't bound for prison.

Everything else seemed small in comparison.

Maybe she would regret not accepting the job in the future, but she knew for sure she'd regret not staying in Sicily and trying to make this work. She still had so much to accomplish here.

She realized after the call ended that she had two more messages. One was from Brina, asking how things were going. She'd respond to that soon. The second was from ...

Wow.

Michael Breckenridge, her old high school crush.

She cringed a little. She hadn't even thought about him since a few days after that disastrous high school reunion. It felt like a lifetime ago that he'd been drunkenly propositioning her for a tumble in the coat room. Had that really happened?

She opened the message and read: *Hey babe.*

Ugh. What about their last interaction made him think she was even remotely interested? She hovered her finger over the "Block" button, but then decided that the last part of this story hadn't been written. And every story deserved an ending.

She typed in: *What do you want?*

Immediately, he responded with: *Kim and I are getting divorced.*

There was a shocker. She stared at that message for a long time before realizing it didn't matter to her either way. A month ago, such news would've likely propelled her head-first into the coat closet for fifteen minutes she'd regret later. But now, she saw him for everything he was. Absolutely pathetic. *Sorry to hear that.*

She watched the three dots and then: *So let's get together babe.*

She almost laughed aloud. And then she typed in: *Sorry, I live in Sicily now.*

And *then* she blocked the number.

She smiled triumphantly.

She headed downstairs, about to inspect Mason's work, when someone rapped on the door.

Audrey was surprised to find G there with a small, wax-paper-covered bowl. He looked different without his apron or skull cap, his thick dark hair in tousled swirls on his head. Even more handsome. She almost didn't recognize him.

"*Ciao, bella,*" he said with a half-wave. "I felt bad about the way I spoke to you before. I was having a bad day and was short with you. I had to let go one of my servers and I was not in good mood. So I come to apologize. Brought you some *ciambotta.*"

She clapped her hands excitedly. "I was dreaming of that! But … what are you feeling bad about? I don't remember?"

She did, actually, but it was her own fault for insinuating that he might be somehow involved in Fabri's murder. What did it matter, anyway? That was all water under the bridge.

He laughed a great big belly laugh. "Well, if you don't, I'm not going to remind you!"

She smiled and took the dish from him. "You want to come in? I'm just making lemonade."

He nodded and stepped inside, looking around. "The place, it looks good. It's …" His eyes narrowed upon Mason, who was crouched in the stairwell with the railing. "*Scuzi.* I didn't know you had company."

Mason turned around and Audrey made the introductions. Was it her or did the two men size each other up like competitors in a dogfight?

There was a moment of awkward silence that Audrey felt compelled to fill. She said, "Mason also has a one-euro house. He's a contractor so he's better at this than I am. And G owns La Mela Verde. Have you been there, Mason?"

Mason shook his head, put a pencil behind his ear, and started measuring the railing with a tape measurer.

"Oh, well, it's great," she said, pouring two glasses, one for each of the men. She handed one to G. "Especially his *ciambotta.* It's like gold."

Mason didn't answer.

G bowed humbly, accepting the praise. "So how are things going? You working hard?"

She shrugged. "They're going. Not as fast as I'd like but I have the bathroom and my bedroom done. So that's good. The place isn't as big as most, so I don't really have too much more to do."

He nodded. "Is small, yes?"

"Yeah. Just the one bedroom."

Just then, Mason let out a curse under his breath. Audrey whirled to him as he growled, "Boston. Can you give me a hand?"

G drained his glass and headed for the door. "I didn't mean to intrude. I'll see you later?"

"Yes. I'll stop by to return your empty dish," she told him.

"Fill it! With one of your American specialties. Just for me, okay?" He winked at her.

She smiled goofily at him, so entranced by his wink that she totally forgot she wasn't much of a cook. American specialties? Did she have anything that would qualify? He probably wouldn't enjoy her usual Kraft dinner with little cubes of cooked ham. Compared to *ciambotta*? She cringed.

Behind her, Mason whistled. "Hello? Hate to interrupt your little Latin lovefest, there, but ..."

She whirled. If it wasn't her, Audrey would've thought he was jealous. "Shut up. What?"

He pointed to the wall. The holes that had been made during her failed attempt at installing the railing were still there, but now they were even bigger. He'd made it *worse*.

"What did you do?"

G turned around at the door, clearly curious, and came to look, too.

"Hey. It's not my fault. I patched up the walls, but it did no good. Because this wall isn't a wall. It's like ... a shower curtain."

She frowned. "A shower curtain?"

He hooked a finger at her, motioning her forward in the stairwell. She stumbled over the steps and when he pointed to one of the holes, she didn't quite understand until she looked more closely at it and realized it wasn't just a dig in the plaster.

It was a big, fat, gaping hole.

She put her eye closer to the opening and squinted into the dark chasm. "What ... where does that go to?"

"I think it's the house next door. Your neighbors."

G whistled.

She felt queasy. So now, not only did she have a hole from the outside going to her bathroom, she also had a hole into the house beside her own. It made sense, they all shared walls, one after the other, like condos, but she hadn't realized just how thin they were, especially since she hadn't actually seen or heard from anyone on that side of her house. In fact, there was a blue set of double doors a few meters up the street, to what looked like a rather grand home, but no one had ever come in or gone out. "Neighbors? What neighbors? I think that house is abandoned, too."

He took a pen light and shone it inside. "Too bad. Looks nice in there."

"Does it?" How was that fair, that next door was a one-euro house, and it was bigger and nicer than hers? They probably even had a backyard. She grabbed the flashlight and started to look herself, until

158

she realized she was peering in what might have been someone else's property. She sighed. "Well, how do I fix it?"

"I think you need to replace the whole wall. This thing's temporary. It's hollow. Like I said. A shower curtain."

She sighed. She still hadn't gotten her license, and the rest of her money wasn't going to go very far. "That sounds expensive."

"*Very*," G chimed in, making it worse.

Mason shrugged. "I wouldn't try to do it yourself."

Just then, there was another knock on the door. Had the whole town come at once to gape at her troubles?

Audrey tucked a lock of hair behind her ear and exhaled slowly. "What else could go wrong today?"

She went back to the door and opened it to find Detective DiNardo, the big macho guy she'd once been so afraid of, cuddling a tiny white Persian with the most adorable little pout on its face. Beside him was a bald, well-dressed older man whom Audrey had never seen before.

Audrey was puzzled, but her eyes were drawn to the cat.

"Oh!" Audrey said, so immediately enamored by the sight that she nearly forgot the detective who was holding her. "Hi! Aren't you the sweetest?"

She immediately petted the animal, which leaned into her hand. When it did, she noticed the telltale cloudiness in its eye and the swollen eyelid.

Her owner said, "I heard that you were a veterinarian? Luna has been sick for three days."

"I am," she said. "But I'm not really allowed to treat animals without my license. I could get in trouble."

She smirked at him.

As they took a step inside, suddenly, Nick hopped down the stairs and stood proudly in the foyer.

Audrey's face fell. She braced herself.

But they didn't make any remark at all.

G and Mason came over, too. The tiny house was getting awfully crowded.

DiNardo asked sadly, "Do you know what's wrong with Luna?"

Audrey got out her medical bag and took the cat into her arms. After a quick inspection, her original suspicions were confirmed.

"Yep. It's just your regular old run of the mill cat conjunctivitis. Very common."

159

DiNardo didn't seem satisfied. It was funny to see the tough man babying his little cat, coddling it, leaning over it like it meant everything to him. "Are you sure?"

"Quite sure. I'd normally prescribe antibiotics to clear it up, but since I don't have a license … I can't help you with that. But it should clear up in a few days on its own."

His distinguished friend suddenly stepped forward and cleared his throat.

"We were hoping to help you, help us," the man said, offering her a tiny cask, just like the one she'd planned to give to Ernesto on that fateful day. "Please accept this olive oil, for prosperity. I am Orlando Falco, president of the Mussomeli town council. We are very happy that you have chosen to purchase one of our beautiful properties and join our little community."

Audrey took the gift. "Thank you. Nice to meet you. I'm happy to be here, too."

"We were talking at our last board meeting about the increase in strays around the town. They're everywhere, and it appears a lot of them are sick, and dying of disease in the streets. We can't have that if we hope to attract more people to our town."

She nodded, remembering the poor cat she'd seen outside La Mela Verde. "Yes, they likely have mange. It's easily treatable, but you have to catch the animals first."

"That's what we're hoping you can help us with," DiNardo said.

She paused, trying to understand.

"You want me to catch stray animals?"

"Oh, no. At least, not totally. We want you to create a shelter, to bring in and care for these animals. You see, we don't have a vet in Mussomeli, and we need you," Falco said. "To take these animals in."

She wondered if she was dreaming.

"Of course, we'll pay for the building. We have a place in mind, in the center of town. It'll likely have to be fixed up, though. It may take a lot of work, which you'd have to do."

She stared back, speechless, unable to catch her breath.

He smiled.

"We need a vet in this town. We need you."

Audrey felt her heart race in her chest as it swelled with excitement. Could this really be happening to her?

He reached into his jacket pocket and pulled out an envelope.

"We rushed this through," he said, handing it to her.

She lifted the flap and peered in the envelope. A single slip of paper was in there. She didn't have to look hard to know it was her license to practice veterinary medicine in Sicily. She would've happy-danced in her foyer-kitchen, had it been bigger and not packed with people.

She started to tear up.

And then she gave everyone around her a great big bear hug, as if they'd all just handed her the license.

They all seemed to turn crimson.

"I'd love to," she said, wiping away tears. "And…it couldn't have come at a better time. I would have had to go home soon. I'm starting to run low on cash."

He smiled. "You will need it! Considering you bought one of the largest homes in town," he said.

"Yes, consider—" She froze. "I'm sorry, what?"

"Yes, one of the largest and most historic. A daunting task for any renovator, but you have the true spirit of adventure, don't you?"

She shook her head. English was his second language, so he'd probably just used the wrong word. "You mean, one of the smallest properties? One of the most run-down, right?"

He shook his head, looking confused.

"No. The *largest*. This property was once owned by a noblewoman in the sixteenth century, who carried on her secret affairs here with a baron who was not her husband, supposedly."

She laughed. Interesting. Yes, this place was a cave, a nice hidey-hole for secret affairs, but she had a hard time believing any noble had ever lived here.

She moved aside and pointed around the place. "She must've had very simple tastes."

Falco looked confused. Then he spotted Mason, standing in the stairwell, holding his hammer. He squinted at him. "*Dio,* what happened here?"

"Yeah," Audrey sighed. "As you can tell, we're having a little railing issue. But Mason here is an expert carpenter, and he's—"

"Where did that wall come from?" The councilman strode toward it, climbed into the stairwell, and shook it. "Who put this here?"

Audrey stared, confused. "What do you mean? Isn't it supposed to be there?"

He motioned to Mason's hammer. Reluctantly, he handed it over. Falco stuck the end of the hammer into the gaping hole to nowhere and pulled, making the whole thing come apart in chunks. Dust and moldy air filled the room, but as it settled, leaving a large hole, natural light poured through the opening.

Falco pointed. "This is *also* Piazza Tre.*"*

"What?" She climbed the steps and peered in the hole, which was now substantially larger.

In addition to the other half of the staircase, there was a large, open, *furnished* room, as large as a ballroom, with massive picture windows and gothic details. Up that side of the staircase, the hall opened to at least another two rooms.

He was right. It was huge.

She stuck her head so far in she almost fell through, craning to see what was down a narrow hallway, under the steps. "Where does that go? That passage there?"

Falco looked at it and shrugged. "To your garden, I'm sure."

Her garden?!?

She shook her head in disbelief.

"Are you sure all this is mine?"

The councilman nodded. "Yes. Quite sure. The person who owned this place prior to you ran into money troubles and likely illegally sectioned part of the house off for renters. That's the part you've been living in. Oh dear, you thought this little closet was your place?"

She sniffled, close to crying. She was speechless.

Her father would've loved this place. He was the one who said that every one of his projects was an adventure. She peered inside the hole again and her heart practically burst at the thought.

Mason smirked at her. "Are those happy tears because you don't own the ugliest house in town anymore, or sad tears because you're going to have to do a lot more in the way of renovations?"

She shrugged. "I'm just so shocked." She wiped the tears from her eyes and smiled at the men. "Yes. Yes, I would be happy to do it. Thank you for the opportunity."

"Wait, wait, wait ..." Mason said, crossing his arms. "Don't you want to think this over? Isn't this biting off more than you can chew? Do you realize what you're signing up for?"

"What do you mean? Of course I do."

He peered in the hole and shook his head. "You're sure? Renovating this huge place *and* a new shelter? You're the one who came to me crying because you thought your shower was trying to kill you. Looks like that was the least of your worries."

"Okay, yes, it's going to be a lot of work. But I have *you*. Right?"

His smirk disappeared.

"And if I have a shelter, and my license, I'll have money to *pay* you for your services."

Mason nodded, conceding. "Now I see where you're going. All right, I agree."

"Plus, we'll get you a special license so that you can keep the fox, too," DiNardo added, sweetening the deal.

As if understanding, Nick brushed up against her ankles.

She grinned and extended a hand to shake.

"I think you've got yourself a new veterinarian."

Their railing-installation plans upended, they instead celebrated with glasses of lemonade. No one seemed in any rush to leave, and she wondered for a minute if they were all moving in.

"Well, it would be rude of me not to show you all around my new home," she said, smiling.

Her smile widened as she looked at the gaping hole in the wall, and they all huddled around her.

She had some exploring to do.

They all climbed through the hole in the wall and looked at the rest of her place.

She was breathless.

It was massive, a palace fit for a queen. She pulled one of the sheets up to reveal an elegant chaise in blue damask. Dusty, but lovely. All of it was a snapshot from another time period, a collection of original, exquisitely crafted things that showed pride in workmanship—ornate doorways and sculpted cornices. It was incredible.

Up a large staircase, another bedroom and a bath, all made with painstaking detail.

All the men whistled at the same time.

Heart thrumming, she tiptoed downstairs, through that narrow hallway, hand trembling as she turned the knob to go outside. To a yard. *Her* yard.

She exited on a grand and gorgeous patio, leading to a massive, overgrown yard, shaded by olive trees, surrounded by ivy-covered walls.

She walked through the grass, hardly believing the feel of *grass* beneath her feet.

She found herself drawn to the wall, to the overgrown ivy, daring to wonder if there could be the view behind it that she had dreamed of.

She gasped at the vista in front of her.

There, before her, flooding her yard, were the most spectacular views of the old castle in the distance, the rolling hillsides, and the vineyards below. Everything was alive and exploding in a riot of color, more beautiful than anything she'd ever seen before. Not for the first time today, she was absolutely awestruck.

This was her yard, her view. This house was *hers*.

The bright Mediterranean sun warmed her face as she turned and looked back at the house. *Her* house. A not-so-little corner of the world that belonged to her.

Sure, it needed work, a *lot* of work, but now she was ready for it. She was her father's daughter, after all.

It was absolutely everything she'd imagined, the minute she'd taken a look at that ad, while sitting on the T in Boston.

Now, she could see herself living here. Making a life here.

Just then, Nick jumped into her arms, as if he wanted to be included in her dreams.

And those dreams were only just beginning.

NOW AVAILABLE!

A VILLA IN SICILY: FIGS AND A CADAVER
(A Cats and Dogs Cozy Mystery—Book 2)

"Very entertaining. Highly recommended for the permanent library of any reader who appreciates a well-written mystery with twists and an intelligent plot. You will not be disappointed. Excellent way to spend a cold weekend!"
--Books and Movie Reviews (regarding *Murder in the Manor*)

A VILLA IN SICILY: FIGS AND A CADAVER is book #2 in a charming new cozy mystery series by bestselling author Fiona Grace, author of *Murder in the Manor*, a #1 Bestseller with over 100 five-star reviews (and a free download)!

Audrey Smart, 34, has made a major life change, walking away from her life as a vet (and from a string of failed romance) and moving to Sicily to buy a $1 home—and embark on a mandatory renovation she knows nothing about.

Audrey is busy working to open the town's new shelter, while also renovating her own problematic home—and dating again. With the help of friends, she begins taking in sick strays. But not everyone in town is grateful for her services, and she soon makes unexpected enemies.

When Audrey gets a tip about an injured dog near the coast and goes to find him—she finds the dead body of a powerful local instead.

Can Audrey, now a suspect, solve the crime and clear her name?

Or will her Sicilian dream fall apart?

A laugh-out-loud cozy packed with mystery, intrigue, renovation, animals, food, wine—and of course, love—A VILLA IN SICILY will capture your heart and keep you glued to the very last page.

"The book had heart and the entire story worked together seamlessly that didn't sacrifice either intrigue or personality. I loved the characters - so many great characters! I can't wait to read whatever Fiona Grace writes next!"
--Amazon reviewer (regarding *Murder in the Manor*)

"Wow, this book takes off & never stops! I couldn't put it down! Highly recommended for those who love a great mystery with twists, turns, romance, and a long lost family member! I am reading the next book right now!"
--Amazon reviewer (regarding *Murder in the Manor*)

"This book is rather fast paced. It has the right blend of characters, place, and emotions. It was hard to put down and I hope to read the next book in the series."
--Amazon reviewer (regarding *Murder in the Manor*)

Book #3-#6 are also available!

Fiona Grace

Debut author Fiona Grace is author of the LACEY DOYLE COZY MYSTERY series, comprising nine books (and counting); of the TUSCAN VINEYARD COZY MYSTERY series, comprising six books (and counting); of the DUBIOUS WITCH COZY MYSTERY series, comprising three books (and counting); and of the BEACHFRONT BAKERY COZY MYSTERY series, comprising six books (and counting).

Fiona would love to hear from you, so please visit www.fionagraceauthor.com to receive free ebooks, hear the latest news, and stay in touch.

BOOKS BY FIONA GRACE

LACEY DOYLE COZY MYSTERY
MURDER IN THE MANOR (Book#1)
DEATH AND A DOG (Book #2)
CRIME IN THE CAFE (Book #3)
VEXED ON A VISIT (Book #4)
KILLED WITH A KISS (Book #5)
PERISHED BY A PAINTING (Book #6)
SILENCED BY A SPELL (Book #7)
FRAMED BY A FORGERY (Book #8)
CATASTROPHE IN A CLOISTER (Book #9)

TUSCAN VINEYARD COZY MYSTERY
AGED FOR MURDER (Book #1)
AGED FOR DEATH (Book #2)
AGED FOR MAYHEM (Book #3)
AGED FOR SEDUCTION (Book #4)
AGED FOR VENGEANCE (Book #5)
AGED FOR ACRIMONY (Book #6)

DUBIOUS WITCH COZY MYSTERY
SKEPTIC IN SALEM: AN EPISODE OF MURDER (Book #1)
SKEPTIC IN SALEM: AN EPISODE OF CRIME (Book #2)
SKEPTIC IN SALEM: AN EPISODE OF DEATH (Book #3)

BEACHFRONT BAKERY COZY MYSTERY
BEACHFRONT BAKERY: A KILLER CUPCAKE (Book #1)
BEACHFRONT BAKERY: A MURDEROUS MACARON (Book #2)
BEACHFRONT BAKERY: A PERILOUS CAKE POP (Book #3)
BEACHFRONT BAKERY: A DEADLY DANISH (Book #4)
BEACHFRONT BAKERY: A TREACHEROUS TART (Book #5)
BEACHFRONT BAKERY: A CALAMITOUS COOKIE (Book #6)